The Ghosts of Stood between Them.

"Oh, Jayne, no wonder my brother fell for you," he murmured into her silken hair. Then she felt Duncan's rejection, his sudden coolness.

His eyes snapping with bitterness, he muttered, "But I'm not another Iain. I'm immune, my dear sister-in-law, something you'd be well advised to bear in mind." He crossed to the door in three long strides and was gone.

Jayne's throat felt constricted and a strange, empty ache suffused her body. Her thoughts wandered unchecked, and at every turn Duncan's cruel black eyes glittered at her in accusation. She could never escape those eyes, not even when, in her imagination, his arms enfolded her once again.

NANCY JOHN

is a former chairperson of the British Romantic Novelist Association. She lives with her husband in Sussex, where they are active conservationists. They also love to travel, researching backgrounds for the novels that have brought her international renown.

Dear Reader,

Silhouette Romances is an exciting new publishing series, dedicated to bringing you the very best in contemporary romantic fiction from the very finest writers. Our stories and our heroines will give you all you want from romantic fiction.

Also, *you* play an important part in our future plans for Silhouette Romances. We welcome any suggestions or comments on our books, which should be sent to the address below.

So enjoy this book and all the wonderful romances from Silhouette. They're for *you*!

Elaine Shelley
Silhouette Books
PO Box 703
Dunton Green
Sevenoaks
Kent
TN13 2YE

NANCY JOHN

A Man for Always

Silhouette *Romance*

Published by Silhouette Books

Copyright © 1981 by Nancy John

Map by Tony Ferrara

First printing 1982

British Library C.I.P.

John, Nancy
    A man for always.—(Silhouette romance)
    I. Title
    813'.54[F]   PS3560.032/

ISBN 0 340 27941 9

Printed and bound in Great Britain for
Hodder and Stoughton Paperbacks, a
division of Hodder and Stoughton Ltd.,
Mill Road, Dunton Green, Sevenoaks,
Kent (Editorial Office: 47 Bedford
Square, London, WC1 3DP) by
Richard Clay (The Chaucer Press) Ltd.,
Bungay, Suffolk

For Helen

ENGLAND, IRELAND
AND SCOTLAND

Fictional places are _italicized_

SHETLAND
ISLANDS

ORKNEY
ISLANDS

Harris
Lewis
OUTER
HEBRIDES—

INNER
HEBRIDES

ATLANTIC
OCEAN

Aberdeen

SCOTLAND

Dundee

Edinburgh

Glasgow

Isle of Kilraven

Craigmond

NORTH
SEA

NORTHERN
IRELAND
Belfast

IRISH SEA

Manchester

Dublin

IRELAND

Birmingham

WALES

ENGLAND

London ★

N
W   E
S

ENGLISH CHANNEL

Chapter One

Her first awareness was of a confusion of muted sounds. Distant voices murmuring unintelligibly, a phone bell ringing somewhere. And from farther off, the shrill cries of winging sea gulls.

As she drifted back to consciousness, the enveloping darkness became lighter, a brightness that hurt her eyes as she let them flutter open. But it was a dazzle of foggy whiteness which offered no clue to her whereabouts.

"So you're awake, Mrs. Stewart!" This was a man's voice, from close beside her . . . soft-pitched and kindly, with the lilt of a Scottish brogue. "I dinna doubt that you'll be feeling very poorly, so just you lie there and take things easy. You were lucky to escape with no more than a few scratches and bruises."

The fog swirled and began to dissolve away like a summer mist before the heat of the sun. A face took solid shape above her, the concerned face of a youngish man with sandy hair and remarkably clear hazel eyes. He was wearing a white coat.

"Where am I?" she asked dazedly, her voice sounding strange to her own ears.

"You're in Craigmond Cottage Hospital," he told her. "You were brought straight here after the crash, Mrs. Stewart, and . . ."

"Crash?" she asked in bewilderment. "What crash?"

"The plane crash, Mrs. Stewart. You don't remember it?"

She shook her head unhappily. "No, I don't remember anything about a plane crash."

"Well, never mind. That's not altogether unusual after an accident, Mrs. Stewart."

"Why do you keep calling me Mrs. Stewart?" she demanded, struggling to sit up in the narrow bed. But the slightest movement sent a dozen throbs darting through her body, and she sank back against the pillows with a sigh.

"Don't you like your married name?" said the doctor in a tone of gentle reproach. "Round these parts, Stewart is a name to be proud of." The corners of his mouth curved into an engaging grin. "It's nearly as good a name as McFadden . . . Sandy to my friends, but Dr. Alexander McFadden officially."

She closed her eyes in an effort to think more clearly. "Let me get this straight," she said faintly. "I've just been in a plane crash, and my name is Mrs. Stewart?"

The doctor's hazel eyes widened in astonishment. "Are you saying that you didn't even remember your own name? Do you not remember anything?"

The answer to his question was no, not a single, solitary thing. But she couldn't bring herself to admit that. It was so stupid! *I just need to pull myself together and get my thoughts clear,* she chided herself. She lay there silently for a few moments, confident that her memory would suddenly click back into place.

But there was still nothing . . . nothing at all beyond this clinically white hospital room, a window to her right through which she could see only an expanse of sky flecked with racing puffs of cloud and, standing beside the bed, the pleasant young doctor who was regarding her with such anxious concern. Panic welled up and engulfed her whole being.

Dr. McFadden laid a gentle hand on her shoulder.

"There now, don't fret, lassie. As I said, a touch of amnesia isn't all that uncommon when there's been a severe shock. I'll prescribe something to help you sleep, and when you awake again you'll be right as rain."

While speaking, the doctor pressed a buzzer on the wall beside the bed. Almost immediately a woman in a dark blue nursing uniform came into the room. Aged about forty, she was light on her feet for someone so buxom. She wore gold-rimmed spectacles, and the brown eyes behind them lit up when she saw that her patient was awake.

"There's a wee problem, I'm afraid, Nurse." Dr. McFadden took hold of her elbow and led her away from the bed. The girl could hear him murmuring an explanation, and when the nurse looked across at her there was an expression of deep sympathy in her eyes.

"You mustn't worry, my dear," she said soothingly. "Just relax now, and it will all come back to you in due course."

The girl shook her head, a movement which immediately set up a fierce throbbing behind her temples. "I can't possibly rest," she protested, "when I don't know about myself. Not anything at all! You can't understand what it's like. So please tell me whatever you can, whatever you happen to know about me. At least that would help a bit."

The doctor and nurse glanced at one another. Then Dr. McFadden nodded his head in agreement, saying, "I'll leave you with Mrs. Gregory, and she can fill you in. Afterward, she'll give you something to help you sleep." He muttered something sotto voce to the nurse, and with another smile at his patient he left the room.

"Now, lassie, where do you want me to begin?" asked Mrs. Gregory, as the door closed behind him.

"Well, for a start please tell me who I am." She faltered. "The doctor called me Mrs. Stewart."

"That's right—Mrs. Jayne Stewart. You were married to Mr. Iain Stewart."

"I *was* married?" gasped Jayne, with a flutter of dread. "Is my husband . . . dead?"

"Yes, my dear, I'm afraid he is."

"You mean, he died in the plane crash?"

"Oh no, Mrs. Stewart. As I understand it your husband died about two months ago, in London. That's where you were both living."

Jayne felt a curious sense of relief. It would have been horror piled upon horror to learn that her husband—she could form no mental picture of his features, hear no echo of his voice—had been killed in the accident from which she herself had escaped. All the same, her husband's death was a very recent happening and she must still be grieving deeply for him. Yet she felt no sense of grief. Apart from her feeling of panic, her emotions were a total blank.

"In the plane . . . was I traveling alone?" she asked.

"Yes, it seems so, lassie. Luckily."

Her tone of voice made Jayne shudder. "You mean that some of the other people in the plane . . . didn't manage to escape? They were killed?"

Mrs. Gregory bowed her head in acquiescence.

"Thank heaven it was only a small aircraft—a shuttle service for the islands. And it was only half full, at that. Besides yourself, there were just three other passengers. And the crew, of course."

"Was I the only one to survive?" asked Jayne, dreading the answer.

"Aye, you were, lassie."

There was a long moment of silence, then Jayne went on timidly. "What was I doing on that plane? You said something about islands. Which islands?"

"Why, the Western Isles."

"You mean . . . Scotland?"

"Naturally." Where else? her expression asked. "You had flown up to Glasgow from London, and you were traveling on to visit your brother-in-law, Mr. Duncan Stewart."

Jayne's heart quickened with gladness. At last, here was some family connection for her to grasp at. "When will I see him?" she asked eagerly. "Will he be coming to the hospital?"

"He's called in a couple of times already, my dear. Only there was no sense in him waiting, and he had plenty to do back home—you've been unconscious for over twenty-four hours. Mr. Stewart is a very busy man, so I promised that I would let him know when you came round, and he'll be here to see you just as soon as he can manage. But it'll take him a wee while to get across the Sound, of course."

"The Sound?"

"The stretch of water that separates us. We're on the mainland here. Duncan Stewart is Laird of Kilraven, an island a few miles offshore. Kilraven has belonged to the Stewarts for centuries. A fine place it is, and Kilraven House is very grand, though it's too large for a man living on his own."

"My brother-in-law isn't married, then?"

11

Mrs. Gregory chuckled. "It's not from want of trying on the part of the eligible young ladies hereabouts, I can tell you! But the Laird of Kilraven is a difficult man to please." She smiled at Jayne apologetically. "I can't really tell you much more than that, lassie. The best thing is for me to pop along to my office now and fetch your belongings. Not that there's much, I'm sorry to say—only the things you had on you when you staggered out of the plane before it went up in flames. Still, the sight of them might serve to jog your memory. And if not, well . . . I'm sure that Mr. Stewart will soon be able to put everything to rights."

Mrs. Gregory bustled out, and was back within a couple of minutes. She carried a white envelope, which she handed to Jayne. "This is all there is, I'm afraid. Your clothes were beyond saving, but we went through the pockets of your jacket carefully. Apart from a hankie, that photograph in there was the only thing we found."

Jayne spilled the contents of the envelope onto the white counterpane in nervous haste. There were two rings . . . a wide, plain gold wedding band, and a narrower gold ring set with a cluster of sparkling diamonds. There was also a gold wristwatch on an expanding bracelet, and a pretty cameo brooch. With only a cursory glance at these items, Jayne gave her attention to the photograph. Snapshot-size, it depicted two men standing together against a background of dark cliffs. They were sufficiently similar in appearance as to be almost certainly brothers, though one was half a head taller than the other. In the color photograph his eyes appeared very dark, ebony black. There was no smile on his lean, craggy face as he gazed directly into the camera, whereas his brother was laughing broadly, obviously enjoying a joke with the person taking the picture.

Jayne became aware that Mrs. Gregory was observing her expectantly. She seemed very disappointed when Jayne asked with a helpless little gesture, "Is—or rather *was*—one of these men my husband?"

"Aye, indeed!" Her stubby forefinger pointed to the laughing man. "That's Iain, and the other is Duncan. It was taken two or three years ago, I'd say, before your marriage."

"I see." Jayne felt a sense of hopeless despair. To be confronted with a photograph of her own husband and her husband's brother, and feel not the slightest stir of recognition . . . it was terrible!

Mrs. Gregory smiled at her and leaned across to plump up the pillows behind her head. Producing two little white pills, she poured a glass of water from the carafe on the bedside locker. "A rest is what you need now, lassie, so I want you to swallow these down. When you wake up again you'll feel a whole lot better. Why don't you put your rings on, lassie? You might find them a comfort."

Obediently, Jayne slipped the engagement and wedding rings on to the third finger of her left hand, where they fit snugly. She felt a momentary uplift of hope at the familiar look of them—an emotion she vaguely associated with loving and caring—but the hope soon died. Beyond this brief, nebulous feeling, there was nothing.

When she was finally left alone, she lay on her side with her gaze riveted on the snapshot that Mrs. Gregory had propped up where she could see it. Presently, as the pills took effect, Jayne began to feel drowsy and to experience the oddest sensation. The man who had been her husband seemed to fade from the picture and it was as though his brother stood there alone . . . a dark, brooding figure against the dark, brooding cliffs. As she drifted into sleep she felt herself held captive by those compelling black eyes. They seemed to bore into her very heart and soul with angry accusation.

Again Jayne surfaced slowly from the void. Her eyelids felt too heavy to open, and her mouth was dry and parched. Blindly, she reached out for the glass of water that she knew was on the bedside locker. It didn't seem to be there, though, and her groping fingers searched in vain.

"Is this what you want?" The voice was harsh, clipped, charged with an undercurrent of disapproval. Jayne felt the tumbler thrust into her hand.

Gripping it tightly, she raised her eyelids and was once again so dazzled by the bright daylight that for a moment she couldn't focus her gaze. When she did, it was the man's eyes she saw first . . . eyes that were indeed as ebony black as the photograph had suggested. And just as in the photograph, those compelling black eyes bore into her with accusation.

Flinching back against the pillows, Jayne said faintly, "You . . . you're Duncan Stewart?"

"I am. And a very different sort of man from my brother, I might add."

She felt tense and nervous under his keen, implacable gaze. Her hand shook so much that the water threatened to spill. He reached out and took the glass from her. Leaning forward, he slipped a hand behind her shoulders and, with surprising gentleness, raised her head from the pillow. "Let me help you, or you'll slop the water all over yourself."

Gratefully, she sipped from the glass he held to her lips. As he released her, his expression was perplexed. "They told me that, physically, you are quite okay. Yet you're trembling like a leaf."

"I'm sorry," she stammered miserably, "but . . . I

know it must sound crazy, but I can't remember anything about myself. Nothing at all."

"So Dr. McFadden explained." His eyes hardened again, with suspicion. "You knew who I was, though, the instant you woke up."

Jayne gestured toward the snapshot that was still propped up on the locker. "I'd seen that, you see—it was found in the pocket of my jacket—and Mrs. Gregory told me which of you was which."

Duncan Stewart picked up the photograph and studied it, his forehead creasing into a frown. "This must have been taken nearly three years ago, before Iain . . ." He broke off, his mouth taut. "It's an excellent likeness of my brother. Did you really and truly not remember him when you were shown this snapshot?"

"No, it didn't mean a thing to me," Jayne said unhappily. She felt tears of shame spring into her eyes.

The granite in Duncan Stewart's expression seemed to soften, just very slightly. "It must be distressing for you, I can see that. I understand they have broken it to you that Iain is dead."

She nodded sorrowfully. "But I don't know how it happened, or . . . or anything. I remember nothing about our life together, or even about my own family."

"You have no family," he stated. "Iain told me that. Some vague second cousins in Australia are your only relatives, but you don't have any contact with them."

Jayne felt even more bereft and alone. He had snatched away a lifeline of hope to which she had been clinging. It would have been such a comfort to find that she had parents, brothers and sisters. They could have been sent for, perhaps, and their loving support would surely have helped her to regain her memory. Was it really true that the one and only person in the world she could count on as family was this arrogant, stern-faced man who seemed to resent her very existence?

"Iain and I must have had friends," she said, rather desperately. "Mrs. Gregory told me that we lived in London, though she didn't say exactly where."

"You lived in Chelsea," he informed her disapprovingly. "Iain told me on the phone that you had insisted on taking a fashionable mews flat there at a ruinously high rental. As for friends . . ." He made a dismissive gesture of contempt. "I doubt if there's a single one of your former friends who would want to know you now."

"Why should you say that?" she flared angrily.

Duncan lifted his shoulders in a shrug. "What happens to the wasps around the honeypot when the honey is all gone?"

"You mean Iain and I had no money?"

"Not a cent. Worse than that, your bank had taken to printing your statements in red ink. You and Iain must have had an orgy of spending to get through the whole of his inheritance in the two years you were married."

Jayne fell back against the pillows. Every word Duncan Stewart uttered fell like such a hammer blow that she was almost afraid to ask him anything more. But she *must* learn all that he could tell her, both about her own life and her marriage to his brother—however unpalatable the truth might be!

She was denied any further opportunity to question him, though, because at that precise moment the door opened and Mrs. Gregory bustled in. "Ah, you're awake again, lassie. And very pale you're looking, too." She turned to Jayne's brother-in-law. "I think you should leave now, if you please, and we'll see about getting some nourishment into this young lady."

"Oh, but . . ." Jayne protested.

"No 'buts,' my dear; you'll do exactly as I say. Tomorrow will be soon enough for you to have a nice long talk with Mr. Stewart. And maybe by then we shall have a better idea of how much longer you'll need to stay in hospital."

Duncan nodded, agreeing. "Dr. McFadden explained to me, Jayne, that it's just a matter of keeping you here to make sure there's no sign of concussion or whatever. He wants to run a few more checks on you. As soon as he's given the all clear, I'll get you moved over to Kilraven."

"Kilraven? That's your island, isn't it?"

"That's right. You'll have peace and quiet there to recuperate and regain your lost memory. When that does happen, though, I imagine that you'll find the peace and quiet of Kilraven a bit too much for your taste."

Mrs. Gregory gave him a reprimanding shake of the head. "Kilraven is a really delightful wee island," she insisted, "and anyone in their right mind would love staying there. Now away with you, Mr. Stewart, and let your sister-in-law rest. It's what she needs above everything."

Rest! Later, when he'd gone, the word seemed to mock Jayne as she listlessly tried to spoon down a little of the excellent Scotch broth she was brought on a tray. The picture that Duncan Stewart had painted of her married life, though frustratingly vague, had been utterly condemnatory. If the only things she could learn about herself were so disagreeable, she thought forlornly, it might almost be better if she never did recover her memory but instead set about making a completely new life for herself. That was crazy, though. One couldn't live without roots of any kind. A person can't suddenly begin life again, as if they'd never had a previous existence, at the mature age of . . . what *was* her age? She didn't even know that.

Next morning, wearing a blue robe that Mrs. Gregory had provided, Jayne sat in an armchair by the open window where she could look out at the view.

Craigmond Harbor lay just below her, a scene of bustling activity. Small fishing boats jostled one another at their moorings, and sea gulls wheeled and shrieked above and around a group of herring girls, clad in aprons and bright headscarves, who were busy with the morning's catch.

Duncan Stewart arrived at nine-thirty sharp, striding briskly into the room. His lean-jawed face against the white polo sweater he wore looked bronzed to the color of fall-tinted beech leaves, and his dark hair was tousled by the wind. "Mrs. Gregory told me that you're in better shape today," he clipped.

Jayne nodded. "In one way, apart from a few bruises, I feel great. But my mind is still a complete fog."

"So she said." Duncan stood regarding her in silence for a moment or two, the expression in his dark eyes unfathomable. Then, abruptly, he pulled up a chair and sat down beside her. "Do you feel up to leaving today, Jayne?"

The suggestion startled her. She'd had no idea that she might be discharged from the hospital so soon. 'I . . . I don't really know," she stammered.

Duncan's mouth curled into a grim smile. "It's what you wanted, isn't it . . . to land yourself on me for an indefinite stay? So why hesitate now that your chance has come?"

"You . . . you're not a very gracious host." She faltered unhappily.

"Would you expect me to be, under the circumstances?" He must have seen the pain in her face, for he added quickly, "I'm sorry, Jayne. That was unfair of me, when you can't remember what the circumstances are. The point is that it will do you no good at all to hang about here in hospital, and where else could you go but Kilraven?"

"Back to London, perhaps?"

Duncan shook his head decidedly. "Dr. McFadden would never allow such a long journey. Anyway, where would you stay in London?"

"You told me that Iain and I have a mews flat in Chelsea."

"Had," he corrected. "I tracked down the agent on the phone yesterday, and learned from him that your lease on the place expired three days ago. So no wonder you came hotfoot up to Scotland."

Feeling swamped by the wretchedness of the situation, Jayne looked at him helplessly. "I . . . I just don't know what to say."

"There's nothing much you *can* say, is there? So you'd better just listen to me. If I'm any judge, you haven't a penny to your name . . . in fact, I wonder how you even scraped up enough money for your ticket. And with all your luggage gone up in smoke along with the plane, you haven't a stitch of clothing. So I propose to make a trip to Fort William to acquire a basic wardrobe for you."

"Thank you," she murmured, embarrassed at having to accept his charity. "Fort William . . . that's some distance away, isn't it?"

Duncan brushed this aside. "By Highland standards, it's almost next door. But don't go imagining that I'll return with my arms full of *haute couture* stuff; I should need to go to Edinburgh for that. Whatever clothes I pick up for you will be of a strictly practical nature."

"That's quite understood. I shan't need very much, anyway. Er . . . shall I make out a list for you?"

"No, you can leave it all to me. But I'd better have your vital statistics, Jayne." His glance swept assessingly over her body. "That robe does nothing to flatter you, but I doubt if my brother would have fallen so hard for a girl with a less than sensational figure. What would you be, thirty-four, twenty-three, thirty-four?"

"Twenty-two waist, actually," she corrected, feeling the color sweep into her face.

"You remembered that without any difficulty," Duncan pointed out, his eyes glinting with suspicion.

It hadn't immediately struck Jayne as strange. "I . . . I just spoke instinctively. If I'd paused to take thought, I probably wouldn't have remembered my measurements."

"Could be." He rose abruptly to his feet. "Well, I'll be off."

"Already?" she cried in dismay. "But I thought we could have a long talk and you'd tell me more about myself, and . . . and Iain."

Duncan shook his head. "No, I'd better get moving. Once you're established at Kilraven, there'll be plenty of opportunity for us to talk. There's nothing else to do on the island in the evenings, apart from watching television and reading. You'll probably be bored to death in less than no time."

"I don't know why you should think that." She bristled.

"No?" His dark eyes narrowed so that she couldn't see whether he was angry or amused. "But then, my dear Jayne, you must bear in mind that for the time being I know you a lot better than you know yourself. It does give me an unfair advantage." He reached the door in two long strides. "Expect me back sometime this afternoon."

Left alone, Jayne rose slowly to her feet and stood before the wall mirror, studying her face yet again. Yesterday she had spent a long time gazing into the small hand glass which, at her urgent request, Mrs. Gregory had brought. But the careful examination of her features had failed to provide the key that would unlock the floodgates of her memory.

The face that stared back at her in the mirror formed a perfect oval, with high cheekbones and a small, slightly pointed chin. Her skin was clear, though slightly flushed at the moment from her encounter with Duncan Stewart. The eyes that gazed back at her were the delicate blue of summer harebells. The only blemishes to tell of her recent ordeal were a penny-size bruise on her left temple and an inch-long scratch just below her jaw. The pale honey-gold hair that tumbled to her shoulders looked somewhat lank, and Jayne decided to ask Mrs. Gregory if she could shampoo it before Duncan returned.

Behind her the door opened, and a cheerful voice quoted lightly, "'Mirror, mirror on the wall, who's the fairest of them all?'"

She turned and gave Dr. McFadden a tremulous smile. "However much I look at my face, nothing seems to click in my brain."

Nodding sympathetically, he came and took hold of her wrist to feel her pulse. "Steady as the Rock of Ages," he pronounced after a moment. "If I cherished any illusions that my sudden appearance would set your heart racing, they are well and truly dashed."

"Mr. Stewart says that you're letting me out of hospital today," she said.

Sandy tilted his head to one side. "I think it's advisable. Much as we shall hate to lose you, bonny

Jayne Stewart, you'll be better away from this clinical atmosphere. Over on Kilraven, you'll have things to help remind you of the past."

"But from the way my brother-in-law spoke," she objected, "it doesn't sound as if I've ever been there before."

"True enough." Sandy gave her an assessing glance, as if wondering how much to say. "The two of them— that's Duncan and your husband—didn't exactly see eye to eye about things."

"I rather guessed that," said Jayne. "Why didn't they get on?"

He shrugged. "They were as different as chalk from cheese, you might say. When the old laird, their father, died—it would be four years ago now—he divided his property between his two sons. Iain had been away at the university in Edinburgh, and after he came back he never seemed to settle here. Of course I don't know the whole story, but I gather that in the end there were so many quarrels and disagreements that Iain sold out his share to his elder brother, and went off to London."

"Where he met me?"

Sandy McFadden nodded. "We all knew that Iain had got himself wed, but none of the details. Duncan kept a tight lip about his brother, though a few rumors did filter through to us."

"What sort of rumors?" she asked quickly.

His hazel eyes clouded and he glanced away from her. "Things always get twisted in the telling. People said that Iain had become rather fond of the good life. . . . And who can blame him? After all, marrying someone with your sort of background he could hardly have suggested that you should settle for a quiet existence on a Hebridean island."

"Why do you say that?" asked Jayne uneasily. "What do you know about my background?"

Sandy's look was apologetic. "Very little, really. Just that you used to be on the stage. And that's not hard to believe," he added with a warm grin. "You've certainly got the looks for it, and the figure."

Jayne at once tried to visualize this new aspect of herself. Had she been a straight dramatic actress, or a singer or dancer, or what? But Sandy shook his head when she fired these questions at him. "Honestly, I don't know any more. I'd tell you if I did."

Later, a young nurse took Jayne along to the bathroom and helped her shampoo her hair. After a blow dry it glinted with warm highlights, a soft, silken frame to her oval-shaped face.

Even though the period of waiting for Duncan's return was broken by the arrival of lunch, the time seemed to stretch interminably. It was as if, Jayne realized, her life could not hope to take on any shape or meaning until he was here with her again. Duncan was her one and only link with all that had gone before. Her one and only link with sanity.

Yet when at long last he did arrive, Jayne was unprepared. Sitting again in her chair beside the window, she spun around in confusion when the door opened and Duncan entered briskly. He dumped two cardboard boxes and a bag on the bed.

"Put these things on for the journey," he told her, "they're good and warm. I'll go and load the rest of the stuff I got for you onto the launch, and come back to collect you in twenty minutes. Okay?"

He was gone again as swiftly as he had come. Having jumped to her feet, Jayne remained unmoving for a full sixty seconds, her heart racing, her head spinning. It was just weakness, of course, the result of the terrible experience she'd been through.

Slowly, she crossed the room and began to open the packages. As she spread his purchases on the bed, she realized that Duncan had thought of everything. She had to concede that, in contrast to his brusque manner, he was a man capable of consideration and understanding.

There was a complete outfit, well suited to the short but breezy sea-crossing ahead of her: a warm, quilted, waterproof anorak in a tan color, a pair of slacks in a darker shade of brown, and a beige turtleneck sweater. There were underclothes, tights and a pair of shoes— smart suede lace-ups with a chunky heel—and a silk headscarf with a Dior label. There was a pigskin shoulder bag, too, of a shade which exactly matched the shoes, and when Jayne opened this she found that it contained a hairbrush and comb, and a makeup kit. A white hemstitched handkerchief was tucked into one of the pockets, and there was also a packet of tissues.

Jayne was filled with wonder that a man such as Duncan Stewart, a man of overbearing arrogance, a man who felt great bitterness toward her, should have applied his mind to the task of dressing her up with such thoroughness and care. Then a glance at her wristwatch alarmed her—already seven minutes had gone by. Her brother-in-law, she knew with a stab of anxiety, would not take kindly to being kept waiting.

Hastily, she slipped off the hospital robe and nightgown and began to dress. The new bra in lace-trimmed satin slid on as if it had been tailor-made to her shape—chosen, she was embarrassed to realize, with uncanny skill. Every item fit her to perfection, adding up to give an outdoor-girl image that ideally suited her features and coloring.

Jayne was ready not a moment too soon. Even as she slipped the makeup kit back into the shoulder bag, Mrs. Gregory came in to say that Mr. Stewart was waiting downstairs in the lobby. "You look really bonny," she declared approvingly, giving Jayne a quick glance up and down. "You'll see, lassie, in no time at all you'll be quite yourself again."

Descending the stairs together they found Duncan talking to Dr. McFadden. Sandy's eyes lit up with appreciation at the sight of Jayne, but Duncan merely gave her a look of cool appraisal. "Was everything satisfactory?" he demanded.

"Very much so, thank you! You didn't overlook a thing."

He shrugged dismissively. "It was hardly a difficult assignment. Well, Doctor, thank you again for all you've done for my sister-in-law. And you too, Mrs. Gregory."

"I'll be popping over to Kilraven in a few days' time," said Sandy, as he shook hands with Jayne. "Just to see how you're progressing."

"Oh, but I don't like to trouble you," she murmured.

He laughed, holding on to her hand a moment or two longer than was strictly necessary. "Believe me, it'll be no trouble. No trouble at all!"

Jayne noticed Duncan give the doctor a frowning look. Then he took her by the elbow and led her outside to a large green Rover that stood waiting.

The drive to the quayside took hardly more than a couple of minutes. As Jayne stepped out of the car, a brisk breeze blowing inshore caught her hair and sent it streaming out behind her. She reached into her shoulder bag for the silk scarf, but as she went to put it on, Duncan held up his hand to check her.

"No, don't cover your head," he said, and added almost grudgingly, "your hair looks magnificent flowing in the wind like that. Like threads of finespun gold."

Chapter Two

Duncan's launch was tied up at the quayside. A stockily-built man wearing a Tam o' Shanter emerged from the wheelhouse and jumped ashore.

"Angus, will you put the car away for me, please," said Duncan. "I shan't be needing it again today."

"Aye, Kilraven, I will indeed."

"This is Mrs. Stewart, my sister-in-law," Duncan added, almost as an afterthought.

"Good day to ye, mistress."

The greeting was polite, but guarded. In the brief scrutiny the man gave her, Jayne was aware of his curiosity. The tale must have gone around of how Iain Stewart's wife had lost her memory in the plane crash. But what else, she wondered with a little shiver, did people in these parts know about her? Little to her advantage, that was certain, to judge from Duncan's curt comments and Sandy McFadden's tactfully chosen phrases.

Duncan leaped lithely to the deck, then turned to give Jayne his hand to assist her down. The fleeting contact sent a curious little shiver running through her. Inside the glassed-in wheelhouse he motioned her to a padded leather seat, then started the motor. He signaled Angus to cast off the lines and eased the launch away from the quay. They rounded the stone jetty, and headed out across the open water.

At first, gazing ahead expectantly, Jayne was blinded by the westering sun, which turned the whole expanse of sea into a dazzling sheet of hammered gold. Then, as her eyes grew accustomed to the brilliance, she discerned a dark shape lying crouched on the waterline—almost like a watchful, waiting cat. Gradually the mysterious shape resolved itself into an island, and as they drew nearer she felt an ache in her throat at the sheer loveliness of it. Etched against the bright glow of the sky, its gently rounded heights looked a luminous bronze color. Soft shades of green mantled the lower slopes, and here and there a little white-washed house peeped out from among the trees. On the rocky shoreline, the waves broke endlessly in a creamy foam.

"How very beautiful it looks!" Jayne said impulsively.

"And so it is," agreed Duncan, adding with fierce pride, "Kilraven is the most beautiful place on earth."

"Why did Angus call you Kilraven, and not Mr. Stewart?" she asked him curiously.

"It's the custom. I am Kilraven, and Kilraven is me. And that is the way it shall always be. I've no intention of becoming one of those absentee landlords who go away to live a life of softness in London or Edinburgh."

"Mrs. Gregory mentioned that the island has been owned by your family for centuries."

He nodded. "Kilraven has been ours since Robert

the Bruce granted it in gratitude for the part the Stewarts played in defeating the English."

Jayne's brain, so useless as a memory bank about herself, readily slotted this into perspective . . . probably from long-ago history lessons at school. "Robert the Bruce. That's about seven hundred years back, isn't it?"

"That's right, and the island has passed down in a direct line right through to the present day."

Seven hundred years! Duncan had cause for pride, thought Jayne. Yet her husband had chosen to give up his share of this glorious heritage in exchange for a sum of money.

Chosen? Was that the correct word? Had Iain been persuaded to quit Kilraven against his better judgment, to sell his birthright for a mess of pottage? Jayne stole a surreptitious glance at Duncan's tall figure standing at the wheel, his powerful legs slightly astride to offset the rolling motion of the launch. He looked so formidable, so aggressive, so arrogant. She could well imagine that for Iain, who seemed to have had a more easygoing nature, there would have been precious little hope of withstanding the tyrannical domination of his elder brother.

And yet . . . to completely abandon a heritage of seven hundred years, to give up all claim to this vision of loveliness they were fast approaching, the enchanted island set like a precious gemstone in the burnished sea. How could Iain ever have brought himself to turn his back on it?

Duncan cut the engine, and they glided neatly to rest alongside a curved jetty which formed a little sheltered harbor. Beyond the narrow strip of bleached pebbles rose a dark cliff face that was very like the one in the photograph. The rock was deeply fissured, and at one spot on the far curve of the bay a silver waterfall cascaded down. Clouds had begun to gather now, and patterns of sunlight and shadow chased across the lovely wild scene.

The only nearby habitation was a small stone house, from which an elderly man emerged and came hurrying toward the launch. He gave Jayne an unsmiling nod of greeting when Duncan introduced them, and set about looping the mooring rope around a granite bollard.

Duncan gestured toward a smart, yellow-painted launch that was tied up farther along the jetty behind a couple of small fishing boats. "Does that mean that Miss McEwan is here, Dougal?" he asked.

"Aye, Kilraven. Took the motorcar, she did, about a half hour since."

Duncan gave a little shrug of resignation. "I'm afraid then, Jayne, that it's got to be the land rover for us. Sorry about that; the road to the house isn't exactly smooth." He turned back to Dougal. "There are some parcels in the cabin. Will you load them into the back for me?"

Five minutes later, with numerous parcels piled into the land rover behind them, they bumped up a rutted track to the cliff top. By now the sun was completely hidden behind a bank of menacing black clouds, and within moments they were assailed by the full fury of a gale. Rain slashed against the windshield and drummed on the roof.

"It can happen like this sometimes," Duncan told her. "And often it will clear again just as quickly. Mind you, it's normal for there to be a wind blowing here, and to me that's one of the things that makes these islands so special. You can breathe fresh air that has blown across three thousand miles of ocean. It somehow gives an extra clarity to everything . . . to colors, to sounds and to scents." Apparently embarrassed by his own enthusiasm, he stopped, but not before Jayne had noticed that when Duncan's eyes were not hooded with suspicion and antagonism, they were far from being ebony black, but were alive with color like glinting jewels.

"You probably think I'm stark raving mad," he said with a bitter laugh. "To your sort of person, the bright lights of London, with the noise and stink of jam-packed traffic and millions of people all herded together, is what life is all about."

Jayne wanted to protest against this scornful delineation of her character. To the woman who sat beside him now in the jolting land rover, a woman whose total memory of life stretched back scarcely more than twenty-four hours, the view of Kilraven as she had seen it from the boat seemed lovelier and more desirable than anything she could conjure up in her imagination. Even the wild elements unleashed around them had a wonderfully exciting, untamed grandeur. But what held her tongue was the thought that in her true self she might indeed be just such a person as Duncan supposed her to be—a sophisticated city girl who had only come to visit her dead husband's brother because she found herself penniless.

Jayne longed with all her heart to emerge from the unreal world she inhabited, this terrible prison of the senses. Yet she was afraid, desperately afraid, to know herself for what she was. And with her returning memory, she would inevitably be faced with grief over her husband's recent death.

Feeling torn in two, she closed her eyes to check the hot tears that pressed against her lids. But she couldn't prevent a few from squeezing out and trickling down her cheek. The next minute she was aware of Duncan thrusting a large white handkerchief into her hand.

"You must still be pretty weak," he said gruffly.

"Only another five minutes, though, and we'll be home. Then you can relax with a nice hot cup of tea and you'll feel better."

Jayne dabbed her eyes, took a deep, shuddering breath, and felt a little calmer. She hesitated, then asked in a small voice, "Who is Miss McEwan?"

Staring straight ahead, Duncan replied tonelessly, "Fiona is . . . a friend of mine."

Jayne waited, but he wasn't going to expand on that laconic description. What kind of friend was this Fiona? she wondered. One of those "eligible young ladies" Mrs. Gregory had spoken of who pursued the Laird of Kilraven? Was Fiona the special one, perhaps, who was making headway with him? If Fiona could arrive uninvited on Duncan's island home in such a familiar manner, and commandeer his car to drive up from the harbor, was she the woman who would finally succeed in ensnaring him?

The road before them suddenly left the storm-swept heath and plunged into conifer woods. As Duncan changed gear, Jayne caught the resinous fragrance of the pine trees. They descended a series of sharp zigzag turns until she glimpsed a gray slate roof, wet and shining from the rain, and a number of tall chimneys. Yet another turn, and the land rover swept across a flagstoned courtyard, and drew up before the portico of a large mansion.

"Here we are, then," said Duncan. "This is Kilraven House, the ancestral abode."

"It's very impressive," said Jayne, leaning forward and peering up through the windshield at the weathered stone walls and diamond-leaded windows. "It looks terribly ancient, but then I suppose it must have been built when your family was first granted the island by the king."

"Good lord no!" he laughed. "This is the *new* house, which was erected from the ruins of the original castle. It's scarcely more than three hundred years old."

A manservant in black clothes came out through the iron-studded doors. He was carrying a large umbrella, which he thrust open as he hurried across to hold the door for Jayne and give her shelter from the rain. When they were all three safely in the protection of the portico, Duncan performed the introductions.

"This is Callum Blair, Jayne, who, with his wife Isobel, runs the house for me. Callum, this is Mrs. Stewart, my brother's wife."

He was a small man, not much taller than herself, and going bald. His heavy-framed spectacles gave him an owllike appearance. As he nodded a greeting, his face was quite unsmiling. Jayne sensed that like the other two men, Angus and Dougal, whatever he might have heard about her had not been favorable.

"There are some boxes and things in the land rover," Duncan told him. "Fetch them in, will you, and take them up to Mrs. Stewart's room."

"Aye, sir. Er . . . Miss McEwan is here."

"Yes, I'm aware of that. Where is she?"

"In the ladies' parlor, sir. She said it was cosier there. Er . . . she asked for a fire to be lit."

Duncan's eyes flickered. "Excellent! I'm sure that Mrs. Stewart will welcome a nice warming blaze. It's turned quite chilly this afternoon. Bring us some tea, if you please, Callum."

As he led the way through an inner pair of doors, Duncan was pounced on by a couple of magnificent red setters, both quite young. Wagging their long-plumed tails, they gave their master an ecstatic welcome. Jayne automatically put out a hand to pat the one nearest to her, and received a sharp-voiced warning from Duncan.

"Don't attempt to get friendly with the dogs until they're accustomed to seeing you around, Jayne. They're not used to strangers, and they might be a bit touchy."

"Oh, nonsense!" she protested, without taking thought. "Dogs have the intelligence to sort out friends from enemies. Here, boy . . . what's your name, eh?"

"He's called Fyfe," said Duncan. "And the other one's Lady."

Both the lovely creatures had sidled up to Jayne now. She tickled their silken throats and they threw back their heads in sheer delight. Duncan, she noted, was looking on with grudging respect.

Accompanied by the dogs, they passed beneath an arch and came to a great hallway with a lofty vaulted ceiling that was obscured in the shifting shadows of early dusk. There was a long oak refectory table, large enough, Jayne estimated, to seat upward of thirty people. Hanging on the stone walls were armorial bearings, draped flags and crossed swords; and here and there stood helmeted figures garbed in chain mail.

Duncan observed her glancing around and gave a dry laugh. "As you can see, the Stewarts of Kilraven were a bloodthirsty lot. But that was the saga of the Highlands and Islands from the early days of the Picts and Scots . . . feuds and fighting and forming allegiances. Happily that's all over now, and we settle any differences that arise in a rather more civilized manner."

A reference to himself and Iain, perhaps? Jayne had no time to ponder that question, for he was opening a door and ushering her through, the two dogs bounding in with them.

By comparison with the Great Hall, this room was small and intimate. The walls were paneled in oak and glowed richly in the light of silk-shaded sconces. A large Turkish carpet covered the floor, and full-length brocade drapes were drawn against the prematurely fading light. A blazing fire of pine logs on the wide stone hearth banished all sense of chill, and soft music came from a stereo.

At first Jayne had thought that the room was empty. Then as they moved closer to the fire, she became aware of an elegantly dressed woman curled up in a wing chair, looking as luxuriously indolent as a cat. Her eyes were as green as any cat's, too, and just as watchful behind their pretended indifference. She extended a lazy hand toward Duncan, who took it, and bent to touch his lips to her petal-soft cheek.

"So this is the prodigal brother's wife," she drawled, arching her penciled eyebrows.

"Her name is Jayne," said Duncan, and completed the introduction. "This is Fiona McEwan, Jayne. Let me take your coat, and go sit down by the fire."

Jayne chose the sofa, uncomfortably aware of being closely watched by those feline eyes. Fiona, high-heeled shoes kicked off and slender legs tucked up beneath her in the chair, wore a deceptively simple black dress in soft jersey wool that enticingly revealed the swell of her breasts. Gold studs gleamed at her earlobes and there was a tumble of gold chains around her neck—a perfect foil for the gleaming red hair which any man might be forgiven for thinking was merely flicked through with a comb, but which Jayne knew had been arranged with care and forethought.

Beside her, Jayne felt gauche and awkward. The well-cut slacks and sweater that Duncan had provided, which had seemed so right for the breezy sea crossing, were out of place in this elegant drawing room. Her cheeks, she knew, were reddened by the wind and her hair was in a tangle.

Jayne was on the point of asking if she could go to her

room to freshen up, when the door opened and Callum Blair entered, pushing a tea trolley.

"That was quick work, Callum," said Duncan, with an approving smile.

"Tea had been ordered already, sir, by Miss McEwan. We only had to make a larger pot."

As the manservant withdrew, Fiona uncurled herself and sat up, taking over the tea pouring as her right. "Sugar and milk, Jayne?" she inquired in a bright, hostessy voice.

Jayne found that she had to consider a moment before answering. In the hospital, though, she'd added no sugar to her drinks. "I . . . I think it's just milk, please."

"Of course, you're suffering from amnesia, aren't you?" The feline eyes smiled with sweet venom as she handed Jayne a cup. "It could be very convenient for you, under the circumstances."

"I . . . I don't know what you mean." Jayne faltered.

"No?" Slender shoulders shrugged with indifference. "This way, you start off with a clean slate. The past can be written off, so to speak. Isn't that so?"

Seething with resentment, Jayne said, "Do you honestly imagine that I want to go on like this, with no memory at all of my previous life? It's quite horrible; it makes me feel like a nonperson."

"I expect you'll manage, though," Fiona drawled.

Dismayed, Jayne glanced toward Duncan, expecting him to come to her defense. But she found that he was regarding her quizzically, his dark eyes half-veiled. As if, she thought desperately, he too had doubts about the authenticity of her lost memory.

Filled with a sudden, urgent need to be alone, she rose to her feet. "If you don't mind, I'd prefer to go straight to my room."

Duncan rose too, looking faintly surprised. "As you wish."

Jayne followed him to the door, awarding Fiona a chilly nod and receiving a satisfied smile in return. She and Duncan crossed the Great Hall and passed through an archway to the staircase beyond.

In silence they mounted the massive oaken stairway which turned three times before reaching a galleried upper hall. Duncan led the way along a corridor to a door on the right. Entering first, he switched on the lights. "I hope this will suit you, Jayne."

It was of a size with the ladies' parlor downstairs, and luxuriously appointed, a subtle blend of antique and modern. The floor was carpeted in a soft dove gray, with fine rugs strewn about to add color. The furniture was all of carved Scots pine, darkened with the patina of centuries, as was the large four-poster bed . . . the first such bed Jayne had ever seen in her life outside museums. Her drifting thoughts froze. How did she know that? Was this a flash of returning memory?

Duncan had crossed the room and opened an inner door. "Here's the bathroom. You should find everything you need." He glanced at the packages which were neatly stacked on an ottoman between the two tall windows. "It looks as if Callum has brought up all your stuff, and I'll send Isobel straight up to unpack for you."

"I can manage the unpacking for myself, thank you," Jayne murmured. "In fact, I'd prefer it that way."

He nodded indifferently. "Dinner is at eight, if you'd care to rest through till then. But come down for a drink beforehand if you feel up to it."

Instead of leaving, he hovered, regarding her uncertainly. Under his dark, brooding gaze, Jane felt engulfed by a sea of misery. Her situation seemed so hopeless, the future so bleak. She felt a wave of nausea, and suddenly the floor seemed to tilt beneath her and she found herself swaying.

"Are you all right?" asked Duncan. "You look very pale."

Jayne couldn't speak; her throat was too choked with tears. She saw Duncan's sternly chiseled face, those harsh accusing eyes of his, through a swirling mist. . . .

He caught her in his arms as she stumbled, and held her pinned against him. There was a thudding in Jayne's ears of her own rapid heartbeat, and she was aware of his musky male scent, which seemed an amalgam of the great outdoors . . . heath and heather, sea and sun and wind. She was piercingly aware, too, of his lean hard-muscled body pressed intimately to her feminine softness, the viselike grip of those strong arms, the pulsing warmth of him.

"Oh Jayne, Jayne, no wonder that brother of mine fell for you," he murmured into her silken hair. Then, abruptly, she felt Duncan's rejection, his sudden coolness. He took a quick step backward so that Jayne would have fallen if she hadn't clutched at a post of the canopied bed.

His eyes snapping with bitterness, he muttered, "But I'm not another Iain, you'd better understand that. I'm immune, my dear sister-in-law, something you'd be well advised to bear in mind." He crossed to the door in three long strides. "Ring if you need anything," he added curtly, and then he was gone.

Still clinging to the bedpost, Jayne lowered herself carefully into a sitting position. Her throat felt constricted and there was a strange, empty ache suffusing her body. During those bewildering moments in Duncan's arms, she had experienced something that had stirred her to the very core of her being. His embrace had seemed so right, so warm and lovely. Because, perhaps, he was her dead husband's brother? Had she found in Duncan an echo of the love she had known with Iain? Was she turning to Duncan, clinging to him emotionally, because he represented her only link with the previous life she had forgotten?

Feeling utterly drained and exhausted, Jayne lay back on the bed just as she was. The ancient room was pleasantly warm, thanks to modern central heating, and the steady patter of rain against the windowpanes had a soporific effect. Drowsiness overcame her and her thoughts wandered unchecked, hardly taking solid shape or form, except for the pair of cruel black eyes that glittered at her in accusation at every turn. She could never escape those eyes, not even in her imagination when Duncan's strong arms enfolded her and held her close.

Outside, the wind howled in greater fury, but Jayne scarcely heard it. Her eyes filled with tears, which tumbled down her cheeks to dampen the richly embroidered quilt, before the sleep of exhaustion finally swallowed her.

Chapter Three

Jayne was startled by a tap at her door, crisp and authoritative. But before she could stir herself to respond, the door was thrust open and Fiona McEwan walked in. Hastily jumping up from the bed, Jayne tried to straighten her rumpled clothes and scoop back her hair. "I'm sorry, I was . . ."

Fiona's green eyes surveyed her with amusement. "You've been having a nice little weep, from the look of you." She held a glass in each hand. "Here, I brought you a drink. I guessed you could do with one."

"Oh, thanks. Er . . . am I late for dinner?"

"Dinner can wait until we're ready for it!" Fiona kicked the door shut with a backward thrust of her elegantly shod foot. "This seems a good opportunity for us to have a little chat."

Jayne had taken the glass from her. She sipped at it, feeling in need of something to pull herself together, and found that the drink was a fine malt whiskey with a little water added.

"A . . . a chat?" She faltered. "What about?"

Unhurriedly, Fiona strolled over to the dressing table and perched on the padded stool. Studying her face in the mirror and outlining the arch of an eyebrow with one long, slender finger, she drawled, "I think it would be such a pity if certain matters weren't made quite clear to you at the outset. Now, if it's true that you really have lost your memory . . ."

"Can you seriously think that I'd pretend about a thing like that?" Jayne demanded hotly.

"Who's to know?" The lazy eyes surveyed her sardonically in the mirror. "If you *are* pretending you're being awfully clever about it, I grant you that. But then, your stage experience, even in meager parts, must have taught you something."

Bewildered, Jayne burst out, "What reason could I have for pretending that I'm suffering from amnesia? What possible good could it do me?"

"Oh, come off it!" said Fiona in a scornful voice. "When you first decided to try for a handout from your brother-in-law, you can't have rated your chances very high. You must have known what a low opinion Duncan has of you. So after the plane crash you grabbed this golden opportunity to play on his sympathy . . . acting the poor little girl with a lost memory and not a friend in all the world to turn to except him."

"It's not true!" said Jayne angrily. "I never expected anything from Duncan."

In the mirror she saw Fiona's eyes widen in triumph. "How can you possibly know that, if you've really lost your memory?"

Jayne felt dismayed, trapped. She did know the charge Fiona had made wasn't true, but how? She said doggedly, "I just wouldn't do a thing like that. Even if I can't remember the past, I still know how I *feel*. The sort of person I am inside."

Fiona swung around on the padded stool to face her, sinuously crossing one slender leg over the other. "And what sort of person *are* you inside?" she inquired. Then, as if not expecting an answer, she went straight on. "Don't be fooled by Duncan's apparent concern for you. That's just an example of his gallantry when it comes to damsels in distress. But you can't go on playing the invalid for much longer, and the moment Duncan sees through you, you'll be out on your ear."

"I'm not playing the invalid," said Jayne angrily.

"No? Remember, Jayne, I was there when you pleaded so prettily to go to your room. And once up here, I gather, you performed a clever scene by swooning into Duncan's arms. He told me, the poor innocent, that if he hadn't caught you, you'd have fallen to the floor."

"It's true! I suddenly became faint, and . . ."

"No doubt you've had a lot of practice acting in cheap melodramas. Be careful, though, that your performance doesn't get too hammy."

Jayne made a helpless gesture with her hands. "What can I do to convince you that I'm not putting on an act?"

The green eyes narrowed to pinpoints. "That's easy! Keep well out of Duncan's way while you remain here on the island, and after a day or two announce that you're leaving and returning to London. That would convince me. But you've no intention of doing that, have you?"

"But don't you see," Jayne protested unhappily, "talking to Duncan is the only way I'm likely to get my memory back. He can tell me all about his brother, and from Iain's phone calls and letters he must know something about our life together."

"And do you imagine it's going to make pleasant hearing?" Fiona sneered.

"Pleasant or not, I've got to find out."

"So under the pretense of discovering yourself, you'll have some nice long tête-à-têtes with Duncan, all alone with him here at Kilraven House. During which you'll treat him to a maximum dose of your seductive charm and get him thoroughly in your clutches. Is that the plan?"

"Of course not!" said Jayne, shocked. "It was Duncan's suggestion that I should come to Kilraven, anyway."

"With the idea cleverly implanted in his mind by you, I've no doubt. Surely you don't think I can't guess how you worked it? You knew perfectly well that when it came to the crunch, Duncan would never turn his back on his brother's widow. Whatever he thought of Iain, his feeling of family loyalty is too strong."

Jayne felt swamped by the other woman's hostility. Somehow she *had* to make Fiona understand that she'd got it all wrong. With a note of desperation in her voice, she said, "Whatever you choose to think, I won't be staying here a moment longer than necessary."

"Than necessary?" echoed Fiona scornfully. "That's a nice, vague, innocuous sort of term. It could mean anything."

Through gritted teeth Jayne said, "I meant a moment longer than it takes me to recover my memory. And the quickest way for me to do that is to find out all I possibly can about myself. After dinner I shall get Duncan to tell me about Iain, and . . . and our marriage."

"You've got it all very nicely worked out in your mind, haven't you?" said Fiona sarcastically. "A cozy little scene before a blazing log fire with the lights turned down low. Very intimate! I'm sorry to have to dash your hopes, Jayne, but I shall be here too. I'm staying the night."

This news was an unpleasant surprise. It was quite true, Jayne acknowledged, that she had been eagerly looking forward to the first real chance of a talk with Duncan . . . though not without a certain amount of dread, too, about what would emerge.

"Duncan suggested," Fiona went on, her lips curled in a gloating smile, "that it would be more sensible for me to wait until morning when the wind will have lifted."

"But . . . but won't you be expected back?" Jayne faltered. "I mean . . ."

"How touching that you should be so concerned about me," said Fiona ironically. "Just to put your mind at rest, I've already called my parents to say that I'm staying the night with Duncan and won't be home." She raised her whiskey glass and drained it with an air of triumph. "Now, just to show that I'm equally concerned for *your* welfare, Jayne, do I tell Isobel Blair to bring you something up on a tray? I could explain to Duncan that you prefer to remain undisturbed in your room, so as to get a good, long-night's sleep."

From her sense of defeat, Jayne was suddenly roused to anger. How nicely it would suit this other woman to have Duncan all to herself for a cozy evening while she cunningly sowed even more seeds of distrust about his sister-in-law. By what right did Fiona McEwan think she could order the running of this household? She was not the mistress of Kilraven . . . not yet!

"Thank you very much," Jayne said freezingly, her chin held high, "but if I have any messages either for Mrs. Blair or for Duncan, I'll deliver them myself. I don't require an intermediary."

Fiona's green eyes glittered, but she gave a careless shrug. "Suit yourself. I was only trying to be helpful."

"But you see, I don't need any help from you." Jayne marveled at the edge of steel she managed to put into her voice at a time when she felt so wretched and miserable.

Fiona turned on her heel and, without another word, walked out of the room, slamming the door viciously. The instant she was alone, all Jayne's screwed-up courage seemed to desert her. Despairingly, she wondered what she should do. Duncan Stewart was already antagonistic toward her, and with an enemy like Fiona to keep the fires of hostility well stoked, what chance had she of ever winning his respect? And she knew, with a deep inner conviction, that she wanted Duncan's respect.

Pulling herself together, Jayne glanced at her wrist watch and saw to her horror that it was almost seven-thirty. Heavens! Duncan had said that dinner was at eight. Though the meal would be something of an ordeal for her, she refused to hand victory to Fiona by asking for a supper tray in her room.

She turned to the various neatly stacked boxes and packages. She listlessly untied the strings, feeling little interest now in what they contained. Yet as she opened one after the other, shaking the contents free of their tissue-paper wrappings, she grew more and more amazed. What Duncan had called a "basic wardrobe" seemed instead to be a wardrobe fit for a royal princess. She wondered if ever before in her life she could have possessed such expensive garments.

There were skirts, slacks, and sweaters in various colors, all carrying well-known labels; two pairs of jeans; and two jackets, one sheepskin and one black velvet. A large box revealed a warm, feather-light coat in white mohair, and another, a raincoat in a lovely subtle shade of moss green. The pile of opened boxes grew larger . . . shoes and tights and panties, nightwear and a lovely flowing robe of peacock-blue satin. There were dresses, too, suitable for every sort of occasion. One that she mentally reserved for putting on now, for dinner, was a soft crepe in a shade of mauve.

There was no time to put everything away now. Jayne hastily slipped into the bathroom to get washed, taking the fully equipped toilet bag that Duncan had provided. It was a beautifully appointed room in blended tones of pink and cerise, and she felt tempted to linger there and enjoy a long, luxurious hot soak. But that would have to wait till later.

She was stepping into her dress when she paused. Part of the wardrobe Duncan had supplied was an evening gown, a flowing, floating dress in red silk, with a deeply plunging neckline. Why not wear it tonight, to help bolster her fraying morale? If Fiona had come to the island without any intention of staying overnight, she would presumably only have the black dress she was wearing earlier. She looked terrific in it, of course, vibrant and sexy, a woman confidently aware of her assets. But surely a gorgeous red evening gown would put Fiona completely in the shade?

Jayne felt a flush of shame pass over her body. Where was this jealous spite coming from? Was it her true nature revealing itself? Was this the sort of person she would discover herself to be when her memory returned?

Angrily, she cast the red gown aside. It would be absurd to put it on this evening in any case. Obviously, Duncan had only provided it in the event of a formal gathering on Kilraven during her stay, when he would expect his sister-in-law to be suitably attired.

The mauve dress fit Jayne perfectly, molding her breasts and slender waistline and hugging her hips. In fact, the total effect, when she had brushed out her hair and carefully applied makeup, was of a poised, sophisticated young woman—quite at odds with her inner quaking. She lingered a moment longer before the mirror, reluctant to go down and face the others. Then she steeled herself and walked briskly to the door.

As she was leaving the room, a door just along the corridor opened and Fiona came out. She looked startled—and far from pleased—to see Jayne dressed for dinner, but she quickly covered this expression with a sugar-sweet smile. "So you felt well enough to come down after all. How nice. And it's lucky that you bumped into me to show you the way. This house is like a maze, and you really have to know it intimately not to get hopelessly lost."

"I think I would have remembered the way," said Jayne, refusing to be provoked.

"You must have a very good memory, then," Fiona taunted. "At least . . . when it suits you!"

Jayne had been half wondering if they would dine in the splendor of the Great Hall. It was something of a relief to find that a much smaller dining room was to be used, a room which, like the ladies' parlor, flickered warmly from a blaze of pine logs on the broad stone hearth. Duncan was standing before the fire, a glass in his hand. He looked immaculate in a dark suit worn with a cream silk shirt, and Jayne was forced to acknowledge that he was a man most women would think of as disturbingly attractive.

Duncan's eyes swept over her in swift appraisal, and he seemed to approve of what he saw. But he made no comment. Instead, he said, "Fiona thought you might prefer to have a tray sent up to your room."

"I didn't want to be a nuisance," Jayne murmured.

"It would have been no trouble," he insisted.

She wondered with a stab of pain if he meant he

would have preferred her to remain upstairs. "I feel that if I keep to myself, I shall never recover my memory," she said unhappily. "My only hope is to talk to you and find out all I can about myself."

"Why not tell the girl what she wants to know, Duncan?" Fiona put in maliciously. "Give it to her straight. Then perhaps we can be finished once and for all with this silly amnesia business."

Duncan's reply carried only a mild reproof. "I hardly think that this is a suitable time for such a conversation, Fiona."

A third place had in fact been laid for her at the circular table, Jayne was pleased to see; nevertheless, dinner was a wretched meal as far as she was concerned. She had no appetite for the fine fresh salmon steaks nor the tender island lamb that followed. The food was served by Mrs. Blair, a severe-visaged woman whose plump figure was stiffly encased in dark gray. She merely inclined her head in dour greeting when Duncan introduced Jayne.

"Will I serve coffee in the ladies' parlor, sir?" she inquired when she had brought in the selection of cheeses and fruit that completed the meal.

"If you please. And then we'll not be needing you again tonight, Isobel."

"You're far too soft with the servants," Fiona observed as the door closed behind her. "Once they sense weakness, they start taking advantage."

"I think the Blairs serve me very well," Duncan commented.

In the ladies' parlor, Duncan switched on the television. Though the picture was somewhat marred by the storm, it hardly mattered, for Jayne felt certain that neither of the other two was watching the comedy show any more than she was. It was simply a convenient barrier against conversation. In the dancing firelight she covertly watched Duncan's face. It remained stern and unsmiling, even when the studio audience rocked with laughter. His lean jaw was set hard, his hands were clenched, and his whole whipcord frame looked tense. Jayne wondered just what was passing through his mind. She switched her gaze and found that Fiona was staring at her. The withering hostility she saw in those green eyes made Jayne recoil with a shudder.

"If you don't mind," she said abruptly, rising to her feet, "I think I'll go up to bed now. I'm very tired."

Duncan turned to look at her in surprise, as if she had crashed in upon his thoughts. But Fiona said smoothly, with an overlay of charm, "Of course, Jayne. It's not to be wondered at that you're tired. Are you sure you don't need to be shown the way?"

"No, thank you, I shall remember."

"Well, good night then, and we'll see you at breakfast." Fiona spoke as if indeed she was the mistress of the household. As if, Jayne thought bleakly, she and Duncan would not be parted during the night, but would be spending the long hours of darkness in one another's arms. Jayne's footsteps were leaden as she made her way upstairs to her room.

When she switched on the lights she saw that all the clothes, which she'd left strewn around just as she had unpacked them, were now tidily put away. Opening the doors of the fitted wardrobe she found the dresses and skirts and coats all neatly hangered, while the other things were arranged in drawers. It seemed to Jayne like a silent criticism. She felt an urge to ring for Mrs. Blair and explain that her untidiness was caused solely by her anxiety not to be late for dinner. But she could imagine the icy indifference which would greet such an explanation.

A hot bath did little to relax her, and she was just about to climb into bed when she became aware that the moan of the wind had lessened; raindrops no longer spattered the windowpanes. Drawing aside the rose-colored velour drapes, she gazed out at the night.

The tranquil beauty of the scene took her breath away. A huge silver moon floated in a soft blue-black sky between the tattered remnants of storm clouds, and there was a faint powdering of stars. In the distance the wind-whipped sea danced with shimmering light, and beyond it, on the mainland, rose a dark mass of mountains—the Scottish Highlands. The silent peace of the night was underscored by the murmuring pulse of waves endlessly pounding the granite rocks.

Pure, clean, untouched beauty. How could anybody, having lived here, voluntarily abandon it for city life?

Yet that was just what her husband had done—or so everyone insisted. All the people who had spoken to her about him—his brother Duncan, Fiona McEwan, Sandy McFadden at the hospital—had been critical of Iain Stewart.

Iain Stewart . . . the man she must have loved with her whole heart and soul. For it was inconceivable to Jayne that she could ever have married a man with whom she was not deeply in love. She had spent two years of her life as Iain's wife before death had snatched him away. Had her marriage brought her happiness? Or had she, in those two years, faced bitter disillusionment? When she eventually recovered her memory, the truth would be laid bare to her.

Jayne let the drapes fall back into place and moved across to the bed. But not to sleep. She lay awake, listening to the silent house. Listening, she realized, for the sound of Fiona's footsteps.

Would she come alone?

Despite the satin quilt on the bed and the central heating of the room, Jayne felt chilly. But then, she reminded herself, she had been a married woman, accustomed until recently to sleeping with a husband beside her. She was no stranger to the supreme act of love between a man and a woman, yet she might never have known that blissful experience for all the response of her body to the thought of Iain Stewart. She focused her mind on the snapshot she had studied so long and so earnestly at the hospital. She dwelt upon his laughing face and tried to imagine him here now, holding her in his arms.

A shudder ran through her and she was suddenly overcome with a strange, insistent longing, which swelled in intensity until her whole body burned with fever heat. Hope soared in her heart. Perhaps this was the way toward a recovery of her memory—to imagine herself in the act of love with her husband, to imagine their limbs sweetly entwined, his urgency arousing in her a mounting surge of desire. . . .

And then, abruptly, the feeling of excitement and happiness drained from her and she was left trembling and ashamed. That vividly imagined mouth, which sought her lips so demandingly, was not the laughing mouth of her husband. Those eyes which looked into hers so compellingly, so desiringly, were not Iain's laughing eyes. . . .

Jayne made a desperate attempt to escape her treacherous fantasy. But she knew, despairingly, that there was no escape for her. Despite her shame and self-disgust, she was still consumed with a passionate yearning to be held close in the arms of Duncan Stewart.

After a restless, dream-tormented night, Jayne woke to find soft golden sunlight filtering through the curtains. Dazed as if from the effect of some potent drug, she stumbled over to the windows. The sky was a clear, cloudless blue, tinged the palest apricot color in the east, where the sun had risen above the picturesque profile of the hills. The sea, still choppy from last night's storm, glistened with silver light. Jayne glanced at her wristwatch and saw that it was only six-twenty.

Opening the leaded casement, she drew in deep breaths of the sweetly fragrant air. She felt an urge to be out there walking in the heather, to let the crystal brightness of the morning cleanse away the stain of guilt and shame that still lingered from last night.

She dressed hurriedly in denim jeans and a sweatshirt, pulling on the sheepskin jacket. There was a pair of walking shoes, too, which she slipped on. The house was silent as she crept down the corridor. Passing the door which she knew was Fiona's, she paused. Was Fiona alone, or was Duncan in there sharing her bed? Jayne bit her lip and hurried on quickly.

Downstairs, as she crossed the Great Hall, there was a sudden scurry of movement and the two red setters came running up. Jayne decided to take them with her, for it seemed too unkind to go walking on such a glorious morning and leave them behind. She slid back the bolts of the heavy oak entrance doors and slipped outside.

There was a fresh, warm breeze blowing and the dogs reveled in it, prancing about with their silk-soft coats ruffled, their tails proudly pluming behind.

The gardens and grounds of Kilraven House had little in the way of clipped lawns and formal gardens. Flowering shrubs grew luxuriantly on the terraced slopes, and rock plants scrambled over the old stone walls in untamed loveliness. A screen of dark conifers made a handsome backdrop to a clump of bright golden azalea bushes, which drenched the air with their sweet fragrance. Small birds flitted and twittered among the branches, and above Jayne's head the sky was alive with song.

The two dogs disappeared into a stand of young

larches that girded the western boundary of the gardens. Jayne followed them down a path where clusters of wildflowers and violets glistened in the wet grass. She heard a man's deep voice calling the dogs by their names, and a moment later a stranger strode into sight around a bend in the path.

He was a burly man wearing a tartan kilt and tweed jacket, with a Tam o' Shanter covering his iron-gray hair. At the sight of Jayne he stopped abruptly, his bushy eyebrows raised in surprise. "Good day to you, my lady. Seeing the dogs, I thought it was Kilraven himself! Ye must be Mistress Stewart, Mr. Iain's wife?"

"That's right," she confirmed, looking at him inquiringly.

"I'm Robert MacLeod, the laird's factor," he told her with pride in his voice. "His estate manager, as you Sassenachs would say. I served the laird's father, too, just as my father served before me. That's the way it's been for generations on Kilraven, father to son."

"How splendid!" Jayne said sincerely. "I'm glad to meet you, Mr. MacLeod. Isn't it a glorious morning, after yesterday's storm? I just had to come out for a walk."

"Aye, it's a fine bonny morn, indeed it is. Kilraven himself is usually about by this hour. He's late, this day."

Late with good reason, Jayne thought bitterly. Thrusting the painful thought aside, she decided that she could put this chance encounter with her brother-in-law's factor to good use. Robert MacLeod might be persuaded to talk about things that Duncan himself would never reveal to her. "I expect you know," she began tentatively, "that I lost my memory in the plane crash?"

"Aye, indeed, Mistress Stewart, I am aware of that.

Very distressing it must be for ye." His eyes were watchful.

"I'm hoping," she went on, "that by staying here on Kilraven and talking to the people who knew my husband, all the things I've forgotten might come back to me."

"Aye," he said again, noncommittally.

Jayne plunged in without preliminaries. "Will you tell me why it was that Iain left here and went to London? I mean, what went wrong between the two of them?"

"Is it not Kilraven himself to whom ye should be putting that question, Mistress Stewart?"

"But it's awkward for me to ask Duncan, you must see that. Besides," she added, "I would only get *his* side of the story that way."

"You think there's another side, my lady?"

"There are always two sides, Mr. MacLeod," she retorted, holding her anger in check. She was fast discovering that for the people who surrounded the Laird of Kilraven, loyalty was the name of the game!

"You may be right," the factor acknowledged grudgingly. "The truth of the matter is that some men are made for the lonely wild places, and some men, like Iain Stewart, crave the excitement of the cities. The need is so strong in them that they have no option but to go."

"Are you suggesting that my husband left entirely of his own accord?" Jayne demanded. "Wasn't it instead that life here on Kilraven had become intolerable for him?"

Robert MacLeod prodded the ground with the gnarled stick he carried. "I canna be expected to see into another man's mind, Mistress Stewart."

"But you have a shrewd idea, haven't you? Is it not a fact that Duncan Stewart resented his younger brother

. . . resented him having any share of this island? As a result of which he made things so disagreeable for Iain that he was glad to accept a sum of money in exchange for his birthright? Otherwise," she rushed on, "why did my husband never once return to Kilraven? Why did he never bring me to see his old family home?"

"Iain was perfectly free to return to Kilraven at any time, if he had chosen."

"And risk subjecting me, his wife, to a hostile reception?" she flared. "No, Mr. MacLeod, I think the truth is that my husband's brother had made it abundantly clear that *he* was determined to be the undisputed master of Kilraven."

The factor's eyes were suddenly burning with pride and challenge. "But Duncan Stewart is the *laird!* The Laird of Kilraven *is* Kilraven, ye canna separate the two."

It was exactly what Duncan himself had claimed. *I am Kilraven, and Kilraven is me.* Like some feudal nobleman with his downtrodden serfs, Jane thought angrily. Yet despite this outrageously arrogant attitude, Duncan Stewart somehow inspired the unquestioning loyalty of his staff and servants.

The two red setters came frisking up to them, prancing around playfully, their long pink tongues hanging out. Absently, Jayne put out a hand to caress them.

"Ye have a way with the dogs, mistress," Robert MacLeod said with surprise, almost with reluctance.

"I love animals," Jayne smiled, diverted for the moment.

The factor didn't comment. Instead he remarked inconsequentially, "Ye'll have met Miss McEwan?"

Fyfe and Lady must have sensed the sudden withdrawal of Jayne's attention. They looked up at her with reproachful brown eyes.

"Miss McEwan stayed here last night," she replied evenly. "Apparently it was considered too rough for her to return to the mainland."

"Aye, it was a wee mite choppy on the water," he acknowledged.

"I suppose that you're all impatient for the wedding to take place so as to insure the succession?" Jayne flushed as she spoke, wondering if Robert MacLeod guessed that she was probing. She hadn't intended to discuss Fiona with him, but found that she couldn't prevent herself.

"The laird will wed when he has a mind to," was the factor's cautious reply.

"Do you approve of his choice?" she persisted.

"I dinna doubt that whichever lady Kilraven finally chooses will make him a fine and suitable wife."

Jayne glanced away from the scrutiny of those clear gray eyes, which seemed to see too much. "Er . . . is Miss McEwan from a local family?" she asked.

The factor extended an arm, gesturing across the water to a point on the mainland some little way south of Craigmond. "Her father's house is yonder, a grand estate, I'm told."

"So she and Mr. Stewart have known one another all their lives?"

"Oh no, indeed! Sir Douglas McEwan is from Edinburgh, where he was the president of a banking house. He bought Glenardoch on his retirement about four years since. Miss Fiona, though, has only been living there these past few months. Sir Douglas had set Miss Fiona up in her own wee business in Edinburgh—a boutique. But it wasn't successful and Miss Fiona came here to live with her parents."

And promptly found herself the ideal man for a husband, Jayne thought bitterly. *How it would suit an ambitious, calculating woman like Fiona McEwan to queen it as the Laird of Kilraven's lady.* "I suppose," she mused aloud, "that in this part of the world the wealthy people all tend to stick together?"

"There is no great fortune to be extracted from an island such as this," said the factor, surprising her. "Not if the laird is a good and considerate landlord, that is to say. In fact," he went on, giving her a sideways look, "it was Sir Douglas McEwan's money that saved the day when Kilraven was obliged to find the capital to buy out his brother, Iain. The debt of that has been a burden, though the laird paid it off in less time than he was given. He's done some investing, too, and I believe now he'll have no more need to worry about money."

Still, Jayne thought scornfully, there are more ways of repaying a debt than with hard cash. Had marriage between him and Fiona been part of Duncan's bargain with her father? The price of the loan that had given him absolute power in his island kingdom? Maybe in Duncan's eyes, though, the acquisition of such a beautiful woman as Fiona for his wife was not a price to be paid, but an added bonus.

Taking out a silver watch from the pocket of his tweed jacket, the factor said apologetically, "I must go have my breakfast now, Mistress Stewart. A half hour in this fine fresh air brings on a keen appetite, and my wife will have porridge ready for me and a herring sizzling in the pan." He touched two fingers to his brow. "I'll bid good day to ye, my lady."

As Jayne watched his stocky figure striding away through the larch wood, she wondered dismally if she would find a single, solitary friend on this island. In bringing her here, Duncan Stewart had acted only from a sense of duty. He resented her presence, and he was determined to show her no warmth.

Jayne stood gazing out across the Sound, four miles

of wind-tossed water. Over there lay Craigmond, and once she was in the little town she could be quickly transported to anywhere she might wish to go.

But *where?* That was the problem. Bitterly, she had to acknowledge the fact that there was nowhere else she would prefer to be. Despite the lack of welcome she had encountered on this island, despite the anguish that the nearness to Duncan Stewart would inevitably bring her, it was here on Kilraven, and only here, that she felt any sense of belonging.

Chapter Four

With a long sigh Jayne continued to wander, the two dogs prancing along at her side. Her aimless footsteps led her down into ferny glens, through which crystal-clear streams cascaded in torrents of silver spray, and up over windswept heights. And all the while she was drawing nearer to the timeless surging of the sea.

When she came to a headland, she stopped and gave an involuntary gasp of delight. She was looking down into a sandy cove, hemmed about with high cliffs. On the wet rocks below, two gray seals lay basking in the sun, and all around them the seabirds flew and swooped.

With the roar of the crashing waves so loud in her ears, she did not hear the horse and rider approach. She became aware only that Fyfe and Lady had ceased their dog games and were lifting their slender noses to sniff the air. Then they dashed off together, barking furiously. Jayne let them go, knowing that on an island this size they could hardly get lost.

Sitting down against a granite boulder in a little sheltered hollow, she leaned back and closed her eyes, enjoying the sun's warmth on her face. Today, she thought determinedly, I shall insist on a talk with Duncan. I shall elicit some hard facts from him about Iain. About our marriage. And by this evening I shall know the truth.

"So there you are!" grated a voice from above her. "What the devil did you think you were doing, running off like that and hiding yourself?"

Jayne twisted her neck and looked up to see Duncan astride a huge black stallion. Man and horse stood poised on the hillock above her, etched against the brightness of the sky. Duncan's eyes were glittering with fury, and he seemed to Jayne like some demonic apparition.

"I wasn't hiding," she said indignantly, when she finally managed to find her voice.

He dismounted in a single smooth movement, then leaped down to land right beside her. "You're supposed to be recuperating from an unnerving experience," he declared, "not wandering about in the cold of early morning and risking a nasty chill."

"But it's so beautiful," she protested, "and I'm well wrapped up against the wind."

Duncan stared at her belligerently. "You're shivering."

So she was, but not from the cold. His sudden appearance, his nearness to her, had thrown her completely. Jayne couldn't check her wayward emotions and she felt pierced through with longing. She wanted to reach out and touch him, to fondle his crisp dark hair. She longed to feel Duncan's arms about her again, holding her close against him, longed with a burning intensity to feel his lips on hers.

Jayne felt sick with shame that she should experience such feelings for her brother-in-law. Yet wasn't it understandable? she tried to console herself. She was vulnerable and desperately needed emotional support. And here was this man, so like the husband she had loved and lost. Duncan Stewart was taller, broader, darker, sterner than Iain had been, but he was sufficiently like his brother in appearance to awaken vibrant echoes of the love she had known. At least she knew the cause of her shameful weakness. That was something to be thankful for. In future, during the remainder of her time on Kilraven, she would keep a careful guard on herself.

"I only came out for a short stroll," she informed Duncan coolly. "I was awake, and everything out here looked so lovely."

"A short stroll?" he scoffed. "Callum saw you leaving the house with the dogs just after six-thirty. It's now nearly eight-thirty."

Jayne stared at him in amazement. "But that's impossible. I . . . I mean . . ."

"I've been out this past hour searching for you," he said angrily. "I couldn't understand why the dogs didn't come when I whistled for them. I never believed for one moment that you'd have wandered this far from the house. It's nigh on three miles."

"I . . . I didn't realize," she gasped.

"I was worried to death," he went on. "In terrain like this it's easy to have an accident. You might have gone over the cliffs, or slipped into a gully—anything. There are occasionally snakes around at this time of year. You might have disturbed one and got yourself bitten. A snakebite can be very serious if not quickly treated with serum, especially if you had panicked and started to run. . . ."

"I wouldn't have panicked," Jayne said in a small voice. "But thank you for being so concerned about me. I'm sorry I put you to so much trouble."

Duncan stood, regarding her intently, as if trying to read her mind. Eventually he asked, "Can you ride?"

"Oh yes!" she said unhesitatingly.

His tone was sharp with suspicion. "How do you know that you can?"

"I suppose I don't, really," she admitted. "It's just that I *feel* as if I can. I'm quite sure that I love horses, just as I love dogs. That's a magnificent stallion you're riding, by the way. What's his name?"

"Tristram."

"He has very fine lines, and a beautifully healthy coat. And it's obvious that you have someone to groom him who knows what he's doing."

"Yes, my chap Fergus is a good man when it comes to horses." Duncan's dark eyes were speculatively studying her face. "Iain never gave a hint that you were anything but a city sophisticate."

"I doubt if I was ever that," she said slowly. "Not deep down in my heart. This sort of wild, untamed country seems infinitely preferable to me than any crowded city."

She saw a ripple of muscle as his jaw tightened. "I wonder if you'll still feel the same when you get your memory back."

"I'm sure I shall," she insisted. "I mean, I can't imagine feeling any different."

Duncan shook his head doubtfully. "I've always found that a man or woman has to be born to this kind of life to appreciate it properly. And sometimes they don't—even then," he added pointedly.

Like Iain, he meant, who was supposed to have forsaken his island heritage for the city. Jayne felt a tight bud of anger burst within her. "What did you have to do, to drive Iain away?" she demanded.

"You believe that I *drove* him away?"

"Well, didn't you?" She stared back at Duncan challengingly, but it was as if shutters came down over his eyes. His dark hair, blowing in the wind, was revealed by the strong sunlight to be not so much black as a deep rich mahogany brown. A wayward lock had fallen across his forehead, and she felt an urge to reach out and smooth it back with her fingertips.

"It cost me dear when my brother left here," he muttered angrily.

"Oh yes, I know all about that sordid deal," Jayne retorted, swept along by a mood of recklessness.

Duncan's hand shot out and he gripped her wrist savagely. The pain of it seared her skin like a red-hot branding iron. "What exactly is that remark supposed to mean?" he demanded furiously.

She suddenly felt scared, not so much for herself as for Robert MacLeod. Had the factor been talking out of turn in revealing the source of the money with which Duncan had purchased his brother's share of Kilraven? But she had come too far to go back now. "I mean," she said defiantly, "that I know you borrowed money from Fiona McEwan's father to buy off Iain."

"Did Iain tell you that?" He gritted his teeth. "Are you beginning to remember?"

She shook her head despondently. "No, it was your factor. I met him earlier, and . . . and it happened to come out in conversation."

Duncan's expression was now suspicious. "Robbie is loyal, and he's a man of few words. Why should he have volunteered that sort of information?"

"I . . . I was questioning him, you see, and . . ."

"Questioning him about Fiona?"

"Well, yes," she admitted. "And about Iain too, of course. I was hoping that Mr. MacLeod might say something which would help me to remember everything."

"You referred to a sordid deal," Duncan reminded her coldly. "What could Robbie possibly have said that gave you such an impression? Sir Douglas McEwan and I came to a perfectly normal financial arrangement."

"You could have gone to your bank manager," she pointed out, allowing her voice to ring with challenge. "Or had you tried that already, and been refused? A Hebridean island can't be regarded as a particularly safe investment these days."

"Sir Douglas knew his man." Duncan spoke in a dangerously level voice. "He had faith in my ability."

"Or perhaps," Jayne dared to suggest, "his daughter had her eye on the man she wanted for a husband."

The atmosphere was suddenly charged with tension. Jayne trembled inwardly and regretted having taunted the proud, arrogant Laird of Kilraven.

"You are overlooking the fact," he said with heavy irony, "that at the time of the loan Fiona was in Edinburgh. She only came to live here a few months ago."

But Fiona must have known Duncan for longer than that, Jayne told herself. Had the failure of her boutique merely been a convenient excuse for her to come and live with her parents, where she would be almost on the Laird of Kilraven's doorstep?

It was as if Duncan could see right through into her mind. He said scathingly, "Have you some idiotic notion that I'm the kind of man who would allow himself to be manipulated by a woman?"

"I . . . I don't know what you mean."

"Come, Jayne," he mocked, "you know very well what I mean! Haven't you just been hinting that I permitted Fiona to maneuver me into a position where I shall be obliged to marry her?"

Jayne stared at him, feeling a sudden uplifting of her spirits. "Are you saying that you're *not* going to marry Fiona, after all?"

"After all?" he queried, his dark eyes shadowed.

"Well, I thought . . ." she began, and stopped.

"You thought what?"

"I . . . I don't know. I'm a bit confused."

"Indeed you are! But nothing that I have said could have caused your confusion." His eyes challenged her. "Anyway, why should you be so interested in my matrimonial intentions?"

She flushed a deep scarlet. "I'm not!"

"Really? You could have fooled me, Jayne. Why did you ever raise the subject in the first place, if it's of no interest to you?"

She bit her lip. "I . . . I was merely commenting on things as I see them."

The expression on his lean, wind-burned face taunted her. "And that's all there was to it? You didn't have any other motive?"

For a few moments she hung back, feeling cornered and defeated. Then suddenly an impulse made her burst out, "Very well, then! If you must know, Duncan, I was trying to warn you off."

He adopted a look of patient, polite inquiry. "Just let's get this absolutely straight, shall we? According to your claim of a lost memory, the sum total of your knowledge about me and my character has been acquired during the past two days since you regained consciousness in the hospital. Of Fiona McEwan, you know even less. Yet you take it upon yourself to warn me against her. Don't you think that's somewhat presumptuous of you?"

Jayne could have told him what had passed between Fiona and herself upstairs in her bedroom yesterday evening before dinner. It would have made him see Fiona in a somewhat different light. But she remained silent, having no wish to bear tales behind Fiona's back.

Duncan, seeing that she wasn't going to attempt to justify herself, made a move toward the black stallion, which stood waiting on the hillock above them, proud and motionless as a great stone statue. "I think," he said, "that we should both be getting back to the house."

"Oh, yes. Er . . . I'm afraid that I've no idea which way to go now, so if you could just point me in the right direction . . . ?"

"There's no need for that," he said brusquely. "Tristram is a powerful fellow and he'll be able to bear us both without difficulty."

"Oh no," she protested. "I . . ."

Duncan's eyes narrowed to slits. "You told me a few minutes ago that you could ride."

"It's . . . it's not that." She faltered. "I just don't want to put you to the trouble. I can easily walk."

"Allow me to differ with that opinion," he rasped. "You have already walked three miles this morning, on an empty stomach. Considering that you were only discharged from the hospital yesterday it's obvious that you should not overexert yourself."

Jayne unhappily nodded her acquiescence, knowing that he would insist on having his way. Her reason for refusing in the first place had been that she was scared—scared that mounted on Tristram's back in such close proximity to Duncan, the effect he was having on her emotions would be only too humiliatingly apparent. As they scrambled up the rocky outcrop, the dogs scrabbling ahead of them, she took care not to trip or stumble, thereby obliging Duncan to lend her a helping hand. Luckily she felt confident that she would have no problem in mounting the great stallion, and without hesitation she slipped her foot into the stirrup.

It was Duncan's unasked-for assistance that was her undoing. The touch of his hands at her waist—those long fingers of his all but spanning her slender form—completely unnerved her. Jayne gave a little shudder and almost lost her balance.

For long seconds Duncan held her steady, the two of them frozen into stillness. Jayne was acutely aware of the vibrant heat of his body where it pressed against hers. Then, with a smothered groan, he spun her about to face him and engulfed her in his arms.

It was like a glorious feeling of homecoming, to be locked tightly against the hard-muscled wall of Duncan's chest. Everything else was swept from her mind and she exulted in his embrace. She lifted a radiant face to him and his mouth claimed hers in a fierce and passionate kiss. His lips were hard and bruising in their demand, his tongue thrusting through to make free with the secret recesses of her mouth.

Jayne was lost to all awareness of her surroundings. There was only this man whose kiss was transporting her into wondrous realms of ecstasy. Even through the thickness of their clothing, she could feel his heartbeat thudding in tune with hers, each pulse like the beat of some primitive tribal drum. She pressed herself closer, glorying in the surging desire she had unleashed in him.

Duncan, becoming impatient with the barrier of their clothes, slid up a hand to unbutton her sheepskin jacket, and Jayne let out a low moan of rapturous anticipation. Then, in a sudden rush of shame and panic, awareness came sweeping back to her. This was insanity! Whatever was she thinking of, to have let such a situation develop!

"No, you mustn't," she cried desperately, trying to pull away. But Duncan paid no heed, and tightened his grip. Frantic now, Jayne put her fists against his chest and thrust back with all her might.

For a moment it seemed that Duncan would continue to ignore her struggles and overpower her with his superior strength. But then, abruptly, he relaxed his hold and stepped back. Jayne saw with dismay that his face was rock hard and his eyes implacably black. "You almost had me fooled for a minute," he said, the huskiness of his voice betraying his aroused passion.

"I don't know what you mean," she breathed.

"What a charmingly played little scene," he remarked with cruel sarcasm. "That bit where you slipped from the stirrup and fell back against me . . . it was performed with such precision that I imagine you must have rehearsed it over and over again for some film or whatever."

Jayne gasped. "You don't really think that I slipped on purpose?"

His eyes were smiling, but coldly; his voice was tight with anger. "It nearly worked yesterday afternoon, too, when you did such a pretty little swoon. I've got to hand it to you, Jayne, you certainly know how to play on a man's susceptibilities. Being blessed with a beautiful face and a magnificent, sexy body, I suppose you see no reason why you shouldn't put them to good use. Only you'd better beware, my dear, or you might get more than you bargain for! No doubt you found it easy, leading Iain on until he finally proposed to you. But as I told you before, I am not cast in the same mold as my brother."

"That's very apparent to me," she flung at him. "I

would never have married Iain if he'd been the least bit like you! And it's extremely insulting of you to suggest that I led him on."

"How do you know that you didn't," he inquired in a drawling voice, "if you can't remember anything?"

It was so fatally easy for him to trap her, Jayne thought wretchedly. "I just *do* know, that's all," she insisted. "And as for suggesting that I'm the least bit interested in you, it . . . it's utterly absurd."

"If it's so absurd," he countered, "I can only point out that you have the strangest way of demonstrating your lack of interest in a man."

She flushed, but hit back at him furiously. "You don't understand what it's like for me to be living in a world of shadows, with my past a complete blank. All right, so I succumbed to you just now, I won't try to deny it. But is that really so surprising? The way things are, there's not a single soul in all the world to whom I can relate. So I automatically responded to what I thought was a little show of human warmth. I should have known, though, that to you it was purely a sexual impulse, a momentary gratification."

Duncan didn't answer at once, but regarded her with narrowed eyes. Eventually he jerked out the words: "Either way, Jayne, you're playing with fire. . . . And people who play with fire are liable to get burned. You'd better remember that. Now come on, up you get."

Their homeward trek, after Tristram had crested a ridge, lay across meadows that blazed golden with buttercups. Seated in front of Duncan in the saddle, Jayne was agonizingly conscious of his hard thighs pressed against hers, his strong sinewy arms encircling her body as he gripped the reins. She was achingly aware that she wanted this man . . . not for his resemblance to Iain, her husband, but for himself alone.

She knew, with a rising sense of panic, that she must get away from here, leave the island. It was her only hope! But she also knew with a heavy sense of despair that she could never bring herself to quit Kilraven of her own free will. The bitter awareness that Duncan despised her utterly—even while he found her physically attractive—didn't change her feelings about him one iota.

With a catch in her throat, Jayne acknowledged and accepted the truth. She had somehow fallen in love with Duncan Stewart. But this brightly burning love would surely turn to bitter ashes when her memory returned. Once she had recalled all the vivid details of the past, she would feel sick with shame at having turned to the man who had rejected her husband. The man who had virtually driven his younger brother from the family home.

Be that as it may, Jayne only knew that for the present moment she loved Duncan. If he should take her in his arms and kiss her again, as he had kissed her just now, if he should demand of her more than merely a kiss, she doubted whether she would have the strength to resist him. She imagined his lips on hers, crushing her into blissful submission; she experienced, as though it were happening in reality, Duncan's fingers cupped around her breast, and felt her nipple tingling with a delight that was almost beyond bearing. She kept her hands clenched tightly together in Tristram's mane to prevent them from unconsciously straying to stroke the firm thighs between which she was seated.

From Duncan's grim silence she could gain no clue to his thoughts. As they crossed the wide meadows they passed groups of black-faced sheep and the lovely pale gold Highland cattle. Dotted here and there were the crofters' thatched cottages, from each of which a spiral of tangy peat smoke drifted lazily into the bright morning sunshine. Every now and then a man working in the fields or a woman spinning in her doorway would raise an arm to Duncan in greeting, and he would respond. Jayne guessed that when they had ridden past, speculative eyes would be watching until they disappeared from sight.

They were returning on the western side of the island, so different from the east and perhaps even lovelier in its own way. The sea, capped with waves like dancing white horses, was a deep brilliant blue that would surely outmatch the Mediterranean itself. Other islands, which Jayne knew must be many miles distant in reality, looked so distinct and crystal clear as to be almost within reach of her outstretched hand.

"We're nearly home," Duncan muttered at last, breaking the silence that had been growing increasingly tense.

Jayne made no comment, receiving the news with conflicting feelings. Half of her longed for this journey to be over, half of her wanted it to last forever. As they crested yet another ridge of heather-clad slopes, she looked down and saw the roofs and chimneys of Kilraven House spread below them.

Duncan rode his horse past the front entrance of the house to set Jayne down before going around to the stables. "Tell Mrs. Blair what it is you want for your breakfast," he said.

"Shall I order something for you, too?" she inquired, sliding down nimbly before Duncan could attempt to help her. "What would you like?"

"I'll not be having anything just now," he told her brusquely, as he clattered off across the flagstones.

As Jayne entered the Great Hall by way of the portico, she found Fiona. Dressed to go out in a slick, belted white raincoat and black leather boots, she was pacing up and down impatiently. "So there you are!" she said irritably. "I hope you realize what a lot of trouble you've caused. Duncan has been out searching for you for ages."

"And now he's found me," Jayne replied, marveling at the coolness of her tone. "I started out for a walk and went farther than I intended, that's all. It was good of everyone to be so concerned about me, but quite unnecessary."

There was a sort of grudging respect in Fiona's frown. "Don't try to be too clever," she warned, "or you'll come unstuck. Have you decided yet when you're going to regain your memory?"

"I wish it really *was* a matter of deciding," Jayne replied. "It can't be too soon for me."

"Nor me," snapped the other girl. "This pretense is very boring."

Deciding that Fiona wasn't worth arguing with, Jayne sought out Isobel Blair and the kitchen. She had to try several doors before finding the right one. Both the Blairs were there, also a woman who presumably came in daily to clean. From all three of them Jayne received a look that was far from welcoming.

"Could I have some coffee and toast, please?" she asked with a nervous smile.

"Is that all?" asked Isobel Blair sharply. "Will ye not be wanting some porridge and a bit of poached finnie haddie, Mistress Stewart?"

"No, thank you. I don't require anything more than the toast."

"Hsst! That's no way to keep body and soul together." She gave Jayne a resentful stare. "And there's no call for you to come here to the kitchen when you want something, my lady. Just ring the bell wherever you happen to be, and one of us will answer it."

"I was just trying to save you the trouble," Jayne explained.

"It would be better, if you please." The look in the woman's eyes conveyed in no uncertain terms that she resented Jayne trespassing in her part of the house.

Going up to her bedroom to wash and tidy herself, Jayne heard a vehicle start up outside and crossed to the window in time to see the tail end of a large blue car disappearing into the trees. Fiona, no doubt setting off for home. And good riddance to her, Jayne thought viciously.

Returning downstairs, she found the table set for one in the dining room. In addition to the rack of toast triangles and the dishes of butter and marmalade, there was a small quilted cozy. This, when lifted, revealed two brown-shelled boiled eggs. At a sound from the doorway, Jayne turned to see Callum Blair entering with a silver coffeepot and creamer on a tray.

"I told your wife that I only wanted toast," she pointed out.

"Aye, mistress, but the eggs were upon the orders of the laird. He said that it was important that you should get some nourishment inside of you."

"I see." Despite her lack of appetite, Jayne felt a slight warmth at the thought of Duncan's concern for her welfare. "Well then, I'll do my best to eat one of them, at least," she said. "Where is Mr. Stewart, by the way?"

Blair glanced around the table to check that nothing had been overlooked before he answered. "The laird is away just this minute to the mainland with Miss McEwan."

"He's gone *with* her?" Jayne gasped, too startled to hide her dismay.

"Aye, mistress. It is some business he has with Miss McEwan's father, Sir Douglas, I think."

With that Blair turned and paced solemnly to the door, and Jayne was left alone.

Chapter Five

With their master absent, Fyfe and Lady transferred their allegiance to Jayne. They padded after her wherever her wandering footsteps led. Their eager devotion was her only comfort, otherwise she felt utterly wretched and at a loss for what to do.

The morning dragged by at a snail's pace. For a time she explored the grounds immediately surrounding the house. Afterward, she studied the various trophies in the Great Hall. She was staring up at an age-darkened oil painting of some long-past battle when she heard the sound of a car outside. Duncan returning, she decided, and her heart began to thud with excited expectation.

Heedless of discretion, she ran helter-skelter to the lobby, through the portico, and out to the courtyard. The land rover, driven by Dougal, had just come to a halt. Out of it stepped . . . not Duncan, but the lanky figure of Dr. Alexander McFadden. Jayne felt the color drain from her face in disappointment.

"Hi!" he called. Then, as he drew nearer, his smile faded and he regarded her with critical concern. "You're not looking as well as I'd been hoping, Jayne. You're a great deal too pale."

"I'm just tired, that's all, Doctor," she mumbled.

"Indeed, you do look as if you've been overdoing things a wee bit," he reproved her. Then he grinned. "And the name is Sandy, don't forget. Er . . . are you not going to invite me inside?"

"Yes, of course." She turned and began to lead the way. "I wasn't expecting to see you as soon as this, Sandy."

"I wangled a day off," he said with a laugh. "It's a decent time since I had a whole day to myself, and as things are reasonably quiet at the hospital just now, I felt entitled to take one."

"You shouldn't be wasting your free time in coming to see me," she said uneasily.

"I don't call it wasting my time, Jayne," he told her, and there was a richness of meaning in his voice.

Her spirits lifted and she knew the cause. The knowledge that someone felt warmly about her was a wonderful tonic after all the hostility she had faced. She must be on guard, though, not to give Sandy any cause to grow fonder of her than he already seemed to be. "I think this will be the nicest room for us to sit in," she said, opening the door to the ladies' parlor. "My brother-in-law isn't at home just now. Actually, he's gone across to the mainland."

"So I was informed by the old chap who drove me up from the dock."

Jayne gestured toward the portable bar. "Can I offer you something, Sandy?"

"Thanks, I'll have a dram in a few moments," he said. "But first let me run a professional eye over you."

He studied her face carefully, then felt her pulse.

"You're in fine shape physically, Jayne. It's just a matter of not overdoing things for a while, that's all." He gave her a questioning look. "I take it there's been no sign of a breakthrough with your memory, or you'd have come bursting out with the news the instant you saw me?"

Jayne shook her head sadly. "Everything before the time I woke up in the hospital is still a complete blank."

"Well, you'll not help things along by worrying about it, lassie."

"But I can't stop myself worrying. Nobody seems willing to help by talking about my past life. . . ."

"What about me?" he said reproachfully. "I told you what I could about your husband when you asked me."

"I'm sorry, Sandy, I didn't mean you. But my brother-in-law seems to go out of his way to avoid the subject."

"Maybe because it would revive painful memories for him," Sandy suggested. "Possibly he's thinking of your feelings, too."

"I doubt if any consideration for my feelings would restrain Duncan Stewart," she said bitterly. "He seems to have a very low opinion of the girl his brother married."

Sandy regarded her with troubled eyes. "I dinna think he has any right to hold you to blame for Iain's shortcomings."

"What was it Iain did that was so dreadful, anyway?" she asked. "Why exactly did he quit Kilraven? Was it because he *wanted* to go, or because pressure was put on him to leave?"

"I wasn't in the district at the time of his going," Sandy admitted. "But I knew Iain when we were both in our teens. He was always . . ."

"Always what?" Jayne prompted.

Sandy chose his words carefully. "Let's say, unsettled. He used to complain about there being no sort of life in this part of Scotland, and how boring it was living here."

"But most teenagers go through a phase like that," Jayne protested. "It doesn't really mean anything."

"Aye, but with Iain it was like an obsession. He used to swear that the minute he got his hands on some money of his own, he'd be away like a shot."

Had Duncan taken advantage of his brother's restlessness? she wondered darkly. Had he dangled what seemed like an enormous sum of money before the younger man, to tempt him into renouncing his birthright? *I am Kilraven, and Kilraven is me,* he'd declared with such fierce pride. But would that have been quite so wholly true if Iain had still owned a stake in the family properties?

"Do you know, Sandy," she said unhappily, "Duncan still hasn't told me how Iain met his death?"

"It was a car accident," Sandy explained, but Jayne sensed that he was being reticent, and pressed him for details.

"The truth of the matter is that Iain had been drinking heavily," he finally admitted.

Jayne flushed. "And was I with him in the car when it crashed?"

"No, that wasn't the way of it." With a sigh, Sandy went on, "You'll get around to remembering it all in the end, I suppose, so maybe it's better if I tell you now, to prepare you. It seems that you and Iain had made friends with a wild crowd of people, and that night you were on some kind of pub crawl. Heaven only knows how many you'd been to. At the time of the accident your husband had another woman with him, but she was only slightly injured when his car skidded and ran into a brick wall. You were in a car some way behind, with another man."

"It all sounds horribly sordid," she whispered, putting her hands to her face with a shudder. "I don't understand. . . . I must have loved my husband. I would never have married Iain if I hadn't been in love with him."

Sandy gave her an uneasy smile. "They say that love is blind, don't they?"

How true. And was Sandy McFadden himself blind where she was concerned? Jayne wondered. He seemed to be the one and only person who didn't condemn her utterly. But it was very apparent that he was in the process of falling in love with her, so maybe he was incapable of seeing the faults in her character that everyone else seemed to find.

"I don't know what to do," she murmured huskily. "With every hour that passes I get more and more scared of what I shall have to face when I get my memory back. Perhaps it would be best for me to go away from here—now, without delay."

"No!" Sandy almost shouted his protest. "You mustn't even think of leaving, Jayne."

"But you just said that there's nothing wrong with me physically."

"It would be running away," he said. "And you're too fine a person to do that. Better stay where you have friends, to face whatever it is that you have to face."

"Friends?" she echoed bitterly.

"You have *one* friend," he insisted, his hazel eyes melting with tenderness and devotion. "Don't go away, Jayne . . . please."

She looked at him doubtfully, very tempted to accept his advice against her better judgment. But what would Sandy think of her if he knew the real reason that she was so reluctant to go away . . . that she couldn't bear to separate herself from the Laird of Kilraven—a man who despised her utterly?

Sandy gave a sudden exclamation. "I've just had a fine idea. There's soon to be a job vacant at the hospital which would suit you ideally. Our receptionist, Carol McNicol, is having to leave because her husband's firm has just transferred him to Aberdeen. So what do you think, Jayne?"

"But I don't know anything about that sort of work," she protested.

"That doesn't matter. You need to be intelligent, which you are, and aside from that the job requires tact and kindness and a sympathetic attitude toward the patients and their relatives. All fine qualities of which I'm certain you possess in abundance. Will you not consider it carefully? The best thing, I'm thinking, is for you to start building a new life for yourself right now, Jayne. Then when your memory *does* return, you'll have something to cling to. You won't be adrift in a vacuum, if you follow my meaning."

She nodded slowly. "I couldn't expect to continue living here on Kilraven, though."

"It would be easy enough for you to find somewhere in Craigmond. A bedsitter, or a small flat. That wouldn't be a problem."

Tempting as the idea was, the look of eagerness on Sandy's face made her wonder what she would be committing herself to if she agreed to his plan. "Sandy, if I were to take this job, it wouldn't mean . . ." She swallowed nervously and began again. "I'm so confused in my mind that I don't feel I can . . ."

Luckily, he appreciated what she was trying to say. "I realize, Jayne, that you will have to find yourself again before you can give proper consideration to the future," he said softly. "That's perfectly understood. Only . . . well, I'd like to be around when it happens."

"To pick up the pieces?" she suggested, with a rueful little smile.

Sandy shook his head emphatically. "I dinna think you're the kind of person to fall apart, Jayne."

She poured him his drink then and joined him with a smaller one for herself. The glorious golden malt whiskey trickled down her throat deliciously, bringing warmth and comfort.

"When do you have to go back, Sandy?" she asked.

"I told the boatman to return for me at four o'clock. Is that okay?"

"Of course." She stood up and went across to tug the bell rope hanging beside the fireplace. "I'd better let the staff know that you'll be here for lunch."

Sandy grinned engagingly. "I was hoping you'd invite me."

They were served fresh-caught sole fried in butter, with peas and tiny new potatoes. It was exceedingly good, and Jayne found, to her surprise, that she had a keen appetite. "The last time I had sole . . ." she began, then stopped abruptly, her heart thudding. Sandy regarded her expectantly.

"What were you going to say, Jayne?" he prompted after a moment.

She shook her head helplessly. "I don't know. I just had a sudden picture . . . like a camera shutter opening and closing. I was in a restaurant, at a table with a pale green cloth, and there were flowers and candles in a bowl. For a second it was all so clear and distinct."

"Were you with someone?" he asked.

"I . . . I think so; I can't be sure. If only I could get the picture back!"

"Don't try too hard," he advised. "I think it's probable that you'll get more and more of these brief flashes, until things gradually start to string together into a continuous memory."

They returned to the ladies' parlor for their coffee. It had begun to rain by now, and the sky was heavily overcast, but a fire had been lit in their absence, and in its flickering glow the room looked pleasantly cozy. For the first time since coming to Kilraven she felt able to relax, as she listened to Sandy talking enthusiastically about his work at the cottage hospital. Hardly aware of the passing of time, she was astonished when he glanced at his watch and gave a gasp of dismay.

"Good heavens, it's nearly four o'clock already! I must be away now if I'm not to keep the boatman waiting. Er . . . would you ask someone to . . . ?"

"I'll drive you down to the harbor," she said.

"You *can* drive, then?"

"Well, yes . . . I think so." She pictured herself at the wheel of a car. It felt familiar. "Yes, I'm quite sure I can, Sandy."

"Great!" About to get up, he paused and looked into her eyes. "You'll give serious thought to that job at the hospital, Jayne?"

"I will," she promised.

Sandy hesitated a moment, then with a slightly clumsy movement he leaned toward her and touched his lips to hers. It was an undemanding kiss, and Jayne felt a surge of warmth for him, though she knew that it was no more than gratitude for his kindness and support. She allowed his kiss to linger a few moments, sadly aware that Sandy McFadden had no power to stir her inner depths. And never would have.

Behind them the door was flung open and they broke apart in hasty confusion. Jayne swung around to see the tall, arrogant figure of Duncan Stewart standing there, glaring at them furiously. "What the devil is going on?" he demanded in a thunderous voice.

"I was just leaving," said Sandy, jumping to his feet. He looked rather red in the face.

"Indeed! And why, may I ask, are you here at all?"

"I informed you, Mr. Stewart, that I would be coming over to see how Jayne was getting on."

"Is that what you were doing?" The savage sarcasm bit deep. "You didn't wait long to come, did you? And how do you find your patient, Dr. McFadden, now that you have so carefully examined her?"

Sandy threw Jayne a helpless look of apology. "She's getting on fine, Mr. Stewart. It's just a matter of time now."

Jayne stood up too. "I was going to drive Sandy down to the harbor."

"There's no need!" barked Duncan. "Dougal brought me up, and he's having a cup of tea in the kitchen. You can go back with him, McFadden."

Sandy didn't attempt to argue the matter, for which Jayne was grateful to him. "I'll bid you goodbye, then," he said to her, with a warm smile. "And about that job, let me know in a day or two, Jayne. It won't stay vacant long."

"Okay," she said, and added, from a need to show her defiance of Duncan Stewart, "I'll just come with you to the door, Sandy."

The two men exchanged frigidly curt nods when they left the room. As they were crossing the Great Hall together, Jayne whispered, "I'm sorry that he was so rude to you, Sandy. He seems to have a vile temper sometimes."

Sandy gave her a curious sideways glance. "Not to worry, love; it's like water off a duck's back as far as I'm concerned. But I must say, the sooner you leave here and get yourself established on the mainland, the better I shall be pleased." He gave her a disarming grin. "And not merely for *my* sake, in case that's what you're thinking."

Jayne waited with him in the portico until Dougal appeared, then stood waving to Sandy as the car drove off. Returning to the ladies' parlor she felt a strange mixture of anger and timidity. Duncan was standing on the hearth rug, hands linked behind his back. He glowered at her furiously, and in sheer self-defense Jayne hit out at him. "You didn't have to be so rude to Sandy," she said furiously.

Duncan's smile was freezing, like a humorless sneer. "This is *my* house, Jayne, and I shall behave in it exactly as I please. Which is apparently what you feel entitled to do, also."

"If you're thinking that I took too much for granted in inviting Sandy to stay to lunch, then I apologize. But it didn't occur to me that you would begrudge me offering refreshment to a visitor."

"It wasn't the *lunch* I was referring to." He rapped out the words.

"Then what?"

"The way you and McFadden were behaving when I came in, that's what! Perhaps you'll conduct yourselves with rather more restraint in future. That is, if he should ever decide to come here again."

"More restraint!" gasped Jayne incredulously. "Good heavens, Sandy was giving me a little peck on the cheek before leaving!"

"Not on the *cheek,* Jayne!"

"Well, it was nothing more than an affectionate good-bye kiss," she claimed dismissively.

"Anyway," he demanded, "what was that about a job?"

"There's shortly to be a vacancy for a receptionist at the hospital," she told him, lifting her chin, "and I'm going to apply for it."

"Don't be a fool, Jayne, you can't."

"I can and I will," she insisted.

"I won't allow you to!"

"You can't stop me."

He took two quick strides and stood before her. Jayne quailed before the sheer menace of him, immensely tall, towering above her. "What game are you playing?" he rasped.

"I'm not playing a game at all, Duncan. I'm dead serious."

His eyes narrowed and his lean jaw thrust forward. "Is this some kind of blackmail? Are you saying that unless I agree to play ball, you'll make a laughingstock of me by taking some trifling little job at the local hospital?"

"I . . . I don't know what you mean," she stammered.

"You'd better state your terms," he said bitterly. "Just what exactly do you have in mind?"

"For pity's sake," she cried in despair, "can't I make you understand? There's nothing I want from you—nothing!"

"No? Then why did you come rushing all the way up here from London, a place you couldn't be pried away from before except to go vacationing in one of the jet-set resorts? Answer me that! Exactly why were you on that plane?"

Jayne was silent. She had no answer to his question.

There was no triumph when Duncan spoke again, only an intense weariness. "In coming all this way up to the Hebrides, Jayne, you must have been hoping for—expecting—something a damn sight better than a receptionist's job at a small cottage hospital. You were gambling on far bigger winnings than that."

"You're wrong!" she cried passionately. "You make me sound hard and calculating. But I'm not like that."

"How do you know," he asked ironically, "if you can't remember anything?"

"But I know how I feel *inside* myself." She added

stubbornly, "Whatever you say, Duncan, I'm going to apply for that job."

With an impatient shrug, he turned away from her and went to pour himself a drink. "It will do you no good, Jayne, because you won't be hired."

"How do you know I won't?" There was an arrogant confidence in his tone that made her uneasy.

"Because, my dear sister-in-law, I happen to be chairman of the hospital committee."

Jayne gasped. "You mean that you'd block my application?"

He downed his dram of whiskey in one swallow, and leisurely replaced the tumbler on the side table. "Indeed I would!"

"Then I think that you're utterly despicable."

Her abuse had no visible effect on Duncan. "If it's true, as you claim, that you aren't trying to blackmail me," he demanded in a gritty voice, "why are you so anxious to leave Kilraven and take a job in Craigmond?"

What could she answer? She couldn't tell him the truth—that it was essential to remove herself from his virile presence because of the devastating effect he had on her emotions. Even now, when he had given her cause to loathe and despise him, she still longed to be drawn into a kiss of such intoxicating, dizzying passion that everything else was swept from her mind.

"Well, Jayne? I'm waiting for your answer," he said remorselessly.

She sought around wildly for something to tell him. Something plausible that she could hope he would believe. "When my memory eventually returns, whether it's sooner or later, I shall have to set about building a new life for myself. So I might just as well make a start now. Anyway, it will be better for me to have something to occupy my mind, rather than spending my days loafing about here and brooding over what I can't remember."

"There's plenty you could be doing right here in Kilraven," he said coldly.

"Such as what?"

"Since my mother died six years ago, there has been no one to act as the laird's lady. I look after the islanders as well as I can . . . a good deal better, I pride myself, than most other landlords in my position. Even so, there's still a lot that a woman could do to alleviate hardship among the crofters' families—not just in practical terms, but with a readiness to show feminine sympathy and understanding."

Jayne looked at him in astonishment. "But when you get married, Duncan . . ."

"I'm talking about *now*," he snapped. "Today and tomorrow and next week."

"But surely," she objected in a cool voice, "having such an extremely low opinion of me, you can't seriously think that I'm the right person for doing good works on your island?"

"You could be, Jayne. Thinking about other people's problems for a change might help you through the trauma of discovering the truth about yourself."

Always, she thought bitterly, Duncan seemed to throw in some cruelly critical remark. As if he deliberately kept taunting her in order to keep the flame of his hostility burning bright.

What he was concerned about, of course, was his image in the eyes of the local people. He was unwilling to allow his sister-in-law to leave his protection and take a comparatively lowly job at the local hospital. But he was perfectly ready to have her playing Lady Bountiful to the island crofters, because that would reflect on his own credit.

"I can't imagine," she remarked icily, "that the crofters' wives would take kindly to interference from me, considering the way that you've been poisoning everybody's mind against me."

Duncan shrugged impatiently. "It seems to me," he said, a bite in his voice, "that you're looking for excuses, Jayne. Don't you think that in helping other people, you might have a reasonable chance of rehabilitating yourself?"

She shook her head, too confused to think straight. She made an attempt to switch the challenge from herself to him. "Did you settle your business with Fiona's father satisfactorily?"

"I did."

"And when is the wedding to take place?" she flung out recklessly.

He surveyed her calmly through narrowed eyes. "That wasn't on the agenda."

"Really? Fiona must be slipping. I'd have thought she'd want to nail you down."

"You do a lot of thinking, don't you, Jayne?" he remarked scornfully. "Especially about matters that are no possible concern of yours."

"I was merely expressing an opinion," she protested.

"I see. So now I'll reciprocate and express an opinion of my own. If I were you, Jayne, I'd stop trying to analyze Fiona's motivations, and concentrate instead on analyzing my own."

"What do you mean by that?" she challenged edgily.

His gaze met hers in a long, intent look, and when he spoke again the scorn was gone from his voice. "Can't you really remember anything about your life with Iain, and your reason for coming here?"

"No, nothing," she confirmed. "Nothing whatever, Duncan. If only I could make you believe that."

He stood looking at her for long-drawn moments,

then slowly he reached out and laid his hands on her shoulders. "Oh, Jayne, why do you tempt me so?"

A little shiver ran through her, and she felt herself invaded by a strange weakness. "You said that," she murmured shakily, "as if you think I'm deliberately setting out to tempt you."

"Well, aren't you?" he cried, his fingers digging into the soft flesh of her shoulders. "Isn't it every woman's instinctive nature to act the temptress, to make unspoken promises with her body? It's the devilish power that your sex possesses! You have the ability to beguile and bewitch a man which makes him cast all common sense to the winds. The way you're looking at me now, Jayne, half-fearful yet half-brazen, too . . . you know only too well that you've got me helplessly hooked on the end of your line and you're exulting in the knowledge."

"No!" she protested, her voice no more than a husky whisper.

"Do you deny your very womanhood, Jayne? You're tempting me now, this very instant, enticing me to take you into my arms and make love to you."

"I'm not, I'm not!" she cried. But her words carried no ring of conviction. "How can you want to make love to me," she stammered, "when you despise me?"

"It's myself I despise," he muttered thickly.

It was as if they were both trapped in a dream, as slowly, compellingly, he drew her into his arms. Jayne was aware of nothing but her burning need of him. When his mouth came down to cover hers she felt drowned in rapturous delight. It seemed as if liquid fire ran through her veins. His kiss became more intense, more passionate, as if he wanted to devour her, and his tongue stabbed in to claim the warm, sweet intimacy of her mouth.

With a need she could not quench, she tangled her fingers into the crisp dark hair that curled at the nape of Duncan's neck. He drew her still closer and she responded by arching her body against his, molding her flesh to meet his, thrillingly aware of his surging passion.

As though in a trance, she felt Duncan swing her up into his arms and carry her to the sofa, where he laid her down on the velvet cushions and stretched his long length on top of her, and still their lips were locked in a kiss that seemed to extend to all eternity.

"Oh Jayne, Jayne," he murmured brokenly, when at long, long last he released her and drew back a little. "You're so beautiful . . . so infinitely desirable."

She could see his face just above her, clear and distinct when everything else was just a misty blur. She wanted to trace its lean, decisive outlines with her fingertip . . . the straight, well-formed nose, the sun wrinkles around his eyes, the firm mouth and taut jawline. But before she had a chance Duncan was kissing her again, and she was swept along on a fresh wave of intoxicating pleasure until she was almost frantic with longing.

His tweed jacket, rough against her skin, was impeding him, and with an impatient exclamation he drew back and wrenched it off, flinging it to the floor. When he returned to embrace her again, Jayne smoothed her flat palms caressingly over the molded contours of his chest as she twined her arms up around his neck and pressed herself closer.

Her lips felt sweetly warm and sensual from his kisses, her flesh felt voluptuously soft under the crushing weight of his body, and every part of her being felt gloriously alive, gloriously sensitive. When his hand slipped beneath her sweater and tugged open the buttons of her silk blouse, it was what she wanted and made no demur. He pulled aside her flimsy bra and his hand closed over her naked breast, cupping its soft roundness, teasing the tingling nipple with his thumb. She whimpered aloud at such exquisite torture.

Involuntarily, her fingers began to fumble with his shirt where it was tucked in at the waistband, impatient to drag it free. She ran her hands up across the bare skin of his back, silk-soft to the touch, yet rippling with muscled hardness. Then the slamming of a door in another part of the house broke into her trance and she jerked back to an understanding of what was happening.

"No!" she cried, and tried desperately to thrust him back from her, but his weight remained heavily upon her, rendering her powerless to move.

"You can't stop now," he muttered, his voice thick and throaty. "I thought that pathetic routine went out years ago."

"What . . . what routine?" she faltered.

"The blow-hot, blow-cold routine. And heaven knows, you were blowing hot enough just now. Like a raging furnace."

"I . . . I got carried away," she said miserably.

"You can say that again! Come on, Jayne, let's be adult about this. I want you like crazy and you want me. You can't possibly pretend otherwise, not after that display of passion."

"Why won't you understand?" she sobbed. "I'm dead serious. Let me go at once."

"It's not as simple as that, sweetheart," he told her grimly. "I reckon that you've knocked around enough to know that a man can be aroused to the point of no return."

Frantically she began to struggle to free herself, and

for a horrifying space of time it looked as though Duncan would overpower her. Then suddenly it seemed to get through to him that she really meant what she said. He heaved himself up from her and got to his feet, tucking in his shirt. With a deep sense of wretchedness and shame, Jayne sat up and did her best to straighten her disarranged clothing.

"I . . . I'm sorry if I gave you the wrong impression," she murmured unhappily.

"I'd say that you gave me exactly the right impression! So why the cold feet all of a sudden? If you feel too exposed down here, let's go upstairs. Your room or mine? No one will disturb us there."

Jayne felt herself trembling violently, sick with shame and misery. To help give herself confidence, she stood up and went to pour herself a small nip of whiskey.

"Well," he demanded impatiently, "what do you say to my suggestion?"

"Try to see things from my point of view," Jayne begged him. "For two years I was a married woman, accustomed to having a . . . a close and loving relationship with my husband. Then, soon after his death, I get involved in a plane crash, which robs me of my memory so that I can't even remember him. So is it any wonder that I'm feeling lost and . . . and very vulnerable? Surely you can understand why I responded when a man showed what I thought was tenderness for me."

"There was a lot more than tenderness involved—for both of us," he pointed out dryly. "It was desire, my dear Jayne. Raging, white-hot, undiluted desire."

She flushed, but accepted the word defiantly. "Yes, all right—desire. My body must have known physical desire and fulfillment many times . . . with my husband. So I naturally responded when you . . ."

"What you're saying is that you felt sexy, and that

any male would have served your purpose. How far would you have gone with Sandy McFadden, I wonder, if I hadn't arrived back and broken things up?"

"I told you, that was just a good-bye peck. Sandy has . . . well, grown rather fond of me, and I like him too, very much. But just as a friend, nothing more than that."

"So you do have a certain degree of discrimination," he said sarcastically. "I should feel flattered, I suppose, to be included on your shortlist of acceptable males."

Nothing on earth would persuade Jayne to admit the truth—that she had permitted Duncan to go so far in his lovemaking solely because she was in love with him. Quite madly, desperately in love with him. "You must admit, Duncan," she ventured at length, "that you have a close physical resemblance to your brother."

"What on earth has that got to do with it?"

"I would have thought it was obvious. Your face and body must have reawakened certain memories of Iain in my subconscious. Because even though I can't visualize him, it must all still be there, locked away in some corner of my mind."

Duncan was staring at her, his face a mask of fury and disbelief. When he finally spoke, though, his voice belied his angry expression. Somehow it made things ten times worse for Jayne that he did not shout at her, but maintained a steely self-control.

"You have the most brazen nerve that I've ever encountered in a woman, Jayne. You're daring to tell me to my face that while we were in the throes of passion just now, and I was fondly under the impression that you wanted me every bit as much as I wanted you, it wasn't so at all. No, you were busy having yourself a nice little fantasy, with myself cast in the role of your late husband—my own younger brother."

Jayne shook her head mutely. She wanted to protest,

to find some way of justifying herself. But the right words eluded her. Duncan stood looking at her with withering scorn for a few moments longer, then he swung on his heel and strode to the door. His parting shot was flung back over his shoulder.

"And you thought that *you* had the right to call *me* despicable!"

Chapter Six

Jayne debated long and hard whether to ask for a supper tray in her room that evening. Tempting as the idea was, she felt it would be a cowardly way out. The best thing, she decided in the end, would be to go downstairs and remain coolly aloof this evening—and for the remainder of her stay on Kilraven. There was no doubt in her mind that after what had happened, Duncan would allow her to take the hospital job without any further objection.

When she entered the ladies' parlor Duncan regarded her for several long moments, an expression of veiled mockery on his lean, imperious face. His iron self-control had reasserted itself and there were no lingering signs to betray his recent state of unreined passion, nor the bitter anger that had followed her rejection of him.

Jayne had taken a lot of care with her appearance, out of sheer defiance. She was wearing a jade-green dress of textured fabric, flecked with white angora wool. There was a subtly revealing crossover effect at the bosom, and it was molded smoothly around her slender hips, falling to her knees in soft folds.

"You look stunning, Jayne," he remarked at last, somehow conveying the impression that she was being deliberately provocative.

"You chose the dress," she threw back at him with a show of indifference.

"Yes, and I give myself high marks for that. Still, it's the wearing of a garment to advantage that really deserves the credit. But you, of course, have an unfair advantage over other women because you're endowed with a greater share of desirable attributes."

As Jayne crossed the room to take a seat by the crackling pine log fire, she could feel him watching her intently. She was aware of his silent amusement when she avoided the sofa and chose an armchair instead.

She waited until they were seated at the dinner table before broaching the subject that was uppermost in her mind. "About me taking that receptionist's job at the hospital," she began. "I think . . ."

"We've already discussed this, Jayne, and the matter is closed." With calm indifference Duncan reached out and helped himself from the dish of ratatouille.

"But surely . . . I mean, after what happened . . ."

His eyes, across the table, were as cold and hard and ebony black as she had ever seen them. "Nothing has happened to cause me to change my mind," he said tersely.

"But how can I remain here, in your house, now that . . . that . . ."

"You must be more precise, Jayne, if you want me to follow your line of reasoning."

He was doing this deliberately, just to needle her. Her temper flared and she said, "I'll spell it out in words of one syllable, if you like. I'm saying that I can hardly continue as a guest in your home when I know that at any moment you might try to . . . to seduce me."

"If I had *tried* to seduce you, Jayne, I would not have failed! You know that perfectly well."

"It isn't true," she stammered in protest. "I . . . I . . ."

"I wasn't prepared to be a party to the nasty little game you were playing," he interrupted curtly. "It was my decision to quit, not yours, and that's the only reason why you're still virgin territory . . . as far as I'm concerned, that is. But from now on you can be sure of one thing, my dear sister-in-law. However provocative you try to be, however much you dress up that beautiful body of yours—or however little!—you won't persuade me to lay a finger on you again."

"I'm glad to hear it," she retorted. "But that doesn't alter the fact that I'd prefer to work at Craigmond Hospital."

Duncan sighed with weary impatience. "Don't keep on about it, Jayne. You're not taking any job at the local hospital, and that's final. But if you're so anxious to make yourself useful and fill your time, I've told you what you can do as an alternative."

"Yes, play Lady Bountiful for you," she said furiously. "You can't seriously imagine that any of the island women will accept my friendship."

"Respect, Jayne, is something that has to be earned!"

"Do the islanders respect Fiona?" she burst out before she could stop herself.

"That is a matter entirely between her and them."

"And you!" she flung at him.

Duncan let that pass. "Is Dr. McFadden planning to pay you another 'professional' visit?"

"He didn't say. He's expecting me to phone him in the next day or two about the job."

Duncan raised his eyebrows. "You gave me to understand that your decision on that score was made almost at once."

"So it was. I just thought I'd leave it awhile before confirming with Sandy."

"Keeping him on tenterhooks, is that it?" When Jayne went to protest, he continued, "It's all to the good, though, because now you can tell him that your overbearing brother-in-law has refused his permission."

"Oh, I will! I shall make the situation crystal clear, don't worry."

Duncan smiled, entirely unperturbed. "If you imagine that by so doing you will win sympathy from anybody except that besotted young man himself, you're sadly mistaken."

She glared at him bitterly. "The great Laird of Kilraven only has to say the word, and everyone jumps obediently."

"Not *everyone,* Jayne," he said softly. "You yourself are an exception to the rule. You have to be *made* to do what I say."

"You can't *make* me do anything," she cried, in reckless defiance.

Duncan reached over to fill her wineglass, and Jayne noted despairingly that his large, sun-bronzed hand, with its haze of tiny dark hairs, was as steady as a rock. She herself was trembling all over.

"As to that," he stated with infuriating calmness, "we shall see. Shan't we?"

It was a morning of golden brightness, with less wind than any day so far since Jayne's arrival on the island. At breakfast, she had seen nothing of Duncan. Presumably he was already out and about, the two dogs accompanying him.

With the sun shining down warmly from a clear, cloudless sky, Jayne needed no more than a sweater and slacks as she set out to climb the island's central ridge of hills, known as *Beinn Liath Bheag,* Gaelic for the Little Gray Mountain. Crossing a meadow that was bright gold with buttercups, she came to a small stream that gushed through a tiny ravine, overhung with ferns and rowan trees in their flowering white beauty.

As Jayne stood for a moment on a rustic bridge, gazing down into the sparkling, sunlit water, she experienced a quick, flashing vision of another bridge, another stream. In her vision she leaned with her elbows on a handrail, and she felt the presence of a companion—a man. She turned her head to speak to him and suddenly the image was gone . . . snapped out like an electric lamp. She was back in the present moment, hearing the gurgle of the fast-flowing water over its rocky bed, and smelling the sweet, cool fragrance of the misted ferns.

Her heart began to thud, and she found herself fingering her wedding and engagement rings with a feeling of deep sadness. If only she could have clung to that mental picture for a moment or two longer; if only she could have seen her companion on the bridge . . . Iain, of course. It might have sufficed to bring her memory flooding back like a tidal wave. And perhaps, an inner voice asked, overwhelm her with anguish and disillusion? She felt scared now of recovering her memory—she could acknowledge that—yet at the same time she was desperately impatient for it to happen.

Finally cresting a fold of the hills, Jayne stood for a while drinking in the scene of wild loveliness spread before her . . . the glittering sweep of silver-blue ocean, dotted with islands, the nearer ones sharply defined in this crystalline Hebridean light, the more distant ones draped with the softest lilac haze. She breathed great lungfuls of the magical, scent-filled air, and let the warm sunshine play upon her skin. Her lingering sadness dropped away and she felt exhilarated, tingling with vibrant life.

Very faintly, drifting on the breeze, came a sound of music, the skirl and drone of bagpipes. She listened, fascinated. The sound grew more distinct as the invisible piper drew nearer, playing a poignant tune she did not recognize. Reaching her like this, not blaring from the radio, but drifting naturally across this wild and rocky terrain, the music sounded very beautiful. It was a wistful lament that brought a lump to her throat.

She saw a flash of movement on the higher ridge above her, and a man's kilted figure came striding into view. Though only a silhouette against the brightness of the sky, he was unmistakable. What man other than Duncan Stewart would walk so tall and proud on this island? *I am Kilraven, and Kilraven is me!* Yes, she could see the truth of that proud boast now, and understand it well.

The two red setters, tails pluming gracefully in the wind, skirmished about their master as if delighting in his music. Until, as she watched and listened, one of the dogs abruptly vanished from sight and she heard a piercing yelp of pain.

The bagpipes' tune ended with a discordant wail. She saw Duncan glance backward, then leap down from his high position and vanish from her view, the other dog following him. An instant later came another screech of pain.

Galvanized into action, Jayne started running up the steep slope, dodging the loose, sharp-edged rocks with which the ground was strewn. It was farther than she had realized to the top of the ridge. Before she was halfway there she was panting heavily, and her legs felt like lead.

Her lungs screaming with the need for oxygen, she finally topped the rise. Just below her she saw Duncan crouched beside one of the dogs. It was Lady, and Fyfe was anxiously sniffing around them.

"What . . . what's wrong?" she gasped.

Duncan glanced up at her, and she saw a look of relief in his eyes. Not because it was her, of course, but just because she represented help at hand.

"A rock gave way under Lady," he explained. "And as she fell her leg got caught in a crevice. I think there must be a fracture. If I try to lift her, it will obviously hurt. So I'd better stay here with her, and keep her still. I want you to run back to the house—it's the nearest phone there is—and tell Blair to call the vet in Craigmond. He's to drop everything and get over here as fast as Jock Munro's speedboat can bring him. Understand?"

Fighting for breath, Jayne could only manage the one word. "No!"

"What d'you mean, *no?*" he roared. "Don't argue with me, girl, just get going."

She shook her head as she knelt down beside Lady, pushing Duncan out of the way. Astonished, he started to berate her furiously again. Then, as Jayne laid gentle hands on the injured dog, his words died on his lips. Lady's whimpers ceased, and she lifted her lovely furred head and gazed at Jayne with trusting brown eyes.

"I suppose it makes sense that a woman would do better at soothing an animal in pain," Duncan granted, though very grudgingly. He sprang to his feet. "You stay here with Lady, then, and I'll go for help."

"No!" she said again. "Wait!"

There was a ring of authority in her voice that wasn't

lost on Duncan. He stood looking down at her in astonishment, as Jayne, with infinite care, ran probing hands over the dog's sleek body. She felt Lady flinch, but she uttered no sound, and Jayne nodded in satisfaction.

"This is the cause of the trouble," she said, "and I bet it hurts like the very dickens, poor love."

She placed her two hands with great precision, spreading the fingers one by one, acutely sensitive to Lady's reaction. For a moment or two she remained motionless, then with a sudden quick movement she twisted both her hands. There was a clicking sound, and a tremor ran through the dog's body. After a brief hesitation, Lady lifted her head and licked Jayne's hand, as if in gratitude.

"There, you poor darling, you'll be all right now."

"You mean she's okay?" asked Duncan, bewildered.

"She might feel a bit sore for a few days, but it'll soon wear off," Jayne told him confidently.

"But what was the trouble?" he demanded.

"A dislocation of the shoulder joint. Very painful while it lasts, but soon put right. This is where you come in, Duncan. I didn't want you to leave just now, because I need someone to carry Lady back to the house. It's best that she doesn't put any strain on that leg for a little while, and I think she'd be too heavy for me."

"Sure thing." Duncan was looking at her with eyes that were gentle and soft with gratitude. Once again, Jayne felt amazed that she had ever thought of them as black eyes, when in truth they glowed with jewellike colors.

"You know what I thought, back then?" he went on apologetically. "That you were a stupid female panicking in a crisis. I had no idea . . ." Then, with a look of questioning astonishment, he asked, "How did you know what to do, Jayne? You didn't falter a moment, but went straight to it. I just don't understand."

"Neither do I," she confessed. "But when I saw Lady lying there in pain, I somehow just knew that I could help her. It was pure instinct."

Gently, Duncan lifted the heavy dog in his arms, holding her cradled against his chest with the silky head resting on his left shoulder.

"In any event, we're grateful, aren't we, Lady old girl? In fact, Jayne," he added with a grin, "I reckon I'll have a hard job to pry her away from your side in future. The way she looked at you just now, she's going to be your devoted slave forevermore."

Walking back to the house, not very fast because of Duncan's burden, Jayne found to her pleasure that they were talking naturally without the former constant antagonism. The incident had brought a new sense of closeness between them, and Jayne delighted in the feeling. She had picked up Duncan's bagpipes, as his own hands were full, but she found that the odd, spiky shape of the instrument was difficult to manage and kept shifting its position.

"There's an art in carrying the bagpipes," he laughed. "I'll have to teach you."

"I've never before realized how beautiful they can sound in the right circumstances."

"Never before?" he queried.

Jayne shrugged. "I just say things like that without thinking."

"The same as you acted just now, with Lady. You have the knowledge or the skill buried away in your mind, without remembering how you came by it."

"Yes, that's just it," she said, and gave a deep sigh. "If only I could find the key to make everything come back to me."

She felt Duncan's glance linger upon her. Then he

said slowly, "I wonder if you wouldn't be better off if you didn't get your memory back. Not ever! Be the Jayne you are now, and start building from that."

She gave a bitter laugh. "You mean because the old Jayne, the real me, was so unpleasant?"

"I didn't say that," he demurred.

"You didn't need to say it."

They continued walking in silence, a chill between them, but Jayne would not permit herself to be despondent. In an effort to recapture the lovely mood of harmony, she questioned Duncan about the bagpipes. "I suppose," she said, "that it was one of those early Picts or Scots who first invented them?"

"Heavens no, the pipes are far more ancient than that. Nobody can be certain about their exact origins, but there's evidence that they were known in Mesopotamia and Greece, centuries before the birth of Christ. They first came to the Hebridean Islands sometime during the dark ages, from Ireland." He laughed. "You know, not even all Scotsmen appreciate the wailing of the bagpipes. At the battle of Bannockburn the clan Donald, fighting with Robert the Bruce, used the pipes because they considered them 'more hideous than bugles for frighting the enemy.'"

"Well, I don't agree with the clan Donald," Jayne said stoutly. "The skirl of bagpipes well played is a magical sound."

Lady's accident marked the beginning of a happier time for Jayne. It was not true happiness—how could it be, when she still lived in this lost limbo of the mind and dared not make any plans for the future? All the same, if she took each separate moment as it came and didn't let herself worry over what couldn't be changed, she was able to find pleasure and contentment in small things. And somewhere, deep down, she began to cherish the belief that eventually everything would work out right for her.

Duncan's attitude toward her was definitely changed. Gone was the constant suspicion, the scorn and hostility. There could be warmth between them now, and even occasional laughter.

On the next Monday, Sandy McFadden phoned Jayne to inquire how she was. "Have you decided yet about the job?" he asked.

"Not yet," she found herself answering. "Sandy . . . I'm not so sure it would be a good idea."

He gave an impatient exclamation. "Look, Jayne, just because Duncan Stewart is overwhelmed with gratitude to you about his dog . . ."

"You know about that?" she exclaimed.

Sandy chuckled dryly. "It's all round the neighborhood. There's not such a lot happens in these parts that we can afford to neglect an interesting little tidbit like that. However did you know what to do, Jayne? I presume that at some time you must have taken a course in first aid."

"I imagine so."

"Still, what happened doesn't really alter the situation," Sandy went on, and when she didn't immediately confirm this, he added on a note of anxiety, "It doesn't, does it, Jayne? You still feel the same about wanting to get away from Kilraven?"

She sighed. "I suppose so. Only . . . well, I'd hate to rush into something without giving the whole matter proper thought. Couldn't we leave it awhile longer, Sandy?"

"If you must," he said reluctantly. "Look, I might be able to come over and see you for an hour or so tomorrow, how's that?"

"No, don't!" It was said much too emphatically, and she hurried on in a gentler tone, "Just leave me to make up my mind in my own quiet way, Sandy. I promise that I'll be in touch the moment I've come to a decision."

"Okay, if that's the way you want it. But don't forget, Jayne, the job won't stay open indefinitely."

After dinner that evening, with the long brocade curtains drawn against the fast-fading daylight, she and Duncan sat before a fragrant log fire in the ladies' parlor, listening to *Fingal's Cave,* which Mendelssohn composed after a visit to that part of the world a hundred and fifty years ago. Jayne let the lovely, poignant music flow over her, feeling wistfully happy.

She could sense a certain restlessness in Duncan, though. Several times she was aware of him watching her with an expression of veiled puzzlement on his lean, sculptured face. Presently, almost as if overcoming a great reluctance, he rose to his feet and came to stand in front of her chair.

"Jayne," he murmured, his voice deep and husky in his throat.

She said nothing, keeping very still as she looked up and let herself meet his gaze. Her heart was beating wildly and she felt dizzy and light-headed with expectation.

Duncan's face was stern and unsmiling, and it was almost as though he was driven by an inner compulsion he was powerless to fight as he raised her gently, unresistingly, to her feet. With his two hands he cupped the back of her head and drew her slowly nearer, claiming her mouth in a kiss that was long and slow and infinitely sweet.

"Oh, Jayne!" he murmured again, as he drew back. "You're a beautiful witch. You've ensnared me completely, destroyed my peace of mind."

Jayne was achingly aware of him, of the warmth and scent and taste of him. As they stood there, his thumbs erotically stroking the soft skin at the nape of her neck, she felt suffused with a beautiful golden sensation, and it seemed as if every separate cell in her body was tinglingly alive.

The record ended; there was silence in the room now, except for the crackle and hiss of pine logs in the hearth. Duncan drew her closer, his arms encircling her, holding her pressed against the firm contours of his flesh while his lips brushed the silken softness of her hair. With a shudder she felt his body quicken, his urgency growing as he laid a sensual trail of kisses along her brow, her temple, down the curve of her cheek to the smoothness of her throat. He lingered around the little hollows of her neck before coming up again to claim her lips once more.

Jayne was marvelously, deliriously happy, her whole body thrilling to his touch. She felt a delicious sense of intoxication, as if champagne bubbles were coursing through her veins. Although wisdom told her to resist him, she had no will to, no strength. Duncan's hands slid lower, his fingertips tracing the line of her spine and making her shiver with erotic pleasure.

Yet despite the potent urgency of his desire, she was unafraid of him. She was unafraid, too, of allowing her own longings to mount with his. Somehow she knew— knew without conscious thought—that tonight Duncan would expect nothing, take nothing, that was not freely and eagerly given.

Over and over again, between kisses, they murmured each other's names, savoring the sound. "This past hour," he told her shakily, "I've been fighting a losing battle with my feelings. I was afraid that you'd slap me down if I dared to touch you, but in the end I couldn't help myself."

Jayne gazed back at him with a look of adoration,

marveling that the granite-hard features of this man she loved could soften to such tenderness. With each new kiss, with every caressing movement of his hands, she felt a fresh surge of desire quiver through her, and she moaned softly with the sweet, terrible joy of wanting.

And then, as if from some far-off, distant planet, a bell started to ring. A telephone bell.

They both froze, listening, alert to this threat from the world beyond their own tiny heaven. In the utter stillness the bell rang on and on insistently, till suddenly it ceased. Jayne heard a murmuring voice coming across from the Great Hall, then measured footsteps approaching the door.

"Damn!" muttered Duncan, and dropped his arms from around her neck. In embarrassed confusion, Jayne stepped back, her legs weak and shaky. The next instant the manservant, Blair, tapped on the door and entered. He gave them a slightly curious look, but his voice was without inflection as he said, "If you please, sir, Miss McEwan is on the telephone."

"Ah yes!" Duncan gave a brisk nod. "Er . . . switch the call through to me here, Callum, will you?" Then, "No, on second thought, I'll come out to speak to her. I won't be a minute, Jayne."

As the door closed behind him, Jayne was engulfed by a sudden chill that left her shivering. She felt tainted, somehow, sullied. It was uncanny that Fiona should have chosen this precise moment to call Duncan. From *her* point of view, of course, she couldn't have hit upon a better time to keep him from escaping her clutches. But for that sudden interruption, the situation might well have got completely out of hand. Jayne now felt bitterly ashamed that she had let herself go to such an extent.

Ironically, she actually began to feel grateful to Fiona

for having phoned. Jayne could only be thankful now that she had been given the chance to gather her wits and draw back from the brink of the abyss before it was too late.

One thing was certain: she dare not face Duncan again tonight! She had no confidence that she wouldn't succumb to him again, just as easily as before. Even while she railed against herself for her own stupidity, her whole body throbbed with longing for him.

On trembling legs she crossed to the door, opened it quietly and listened. Duncan was still talking on the phone, which was situated in a small lobby off the Great Hall. With luck she could slip past him to the staircase unnoticed, and go up to her bedroom.

But when Duncan found her gone, he would be certain to come in search of her and demand an explanation. Going quickly to the writing table, she considered a moment, then scribbled, *Am feeling rather tired, so have gone up to bed. See you tomorrow.* She propped it up against Duncan's whiskey glass on the small table by his armchair, so that he could not fail to see it.

Fortunately, Duncan had his back turned and he seemed to be listening intently to what Fiona was saying. On tiptoe, Jayne slipped across the hall and through the archway, then up the wide staircase. In another few seconds she was safely in her bedroom, turning the key in the lock. She stood leaning against the door until the painful hammering of her heart eased off.

It was early, not yet ten o'clock; Jayne knew that she wouldn't find peaceful oblivion in sleep for some time. She went to the window and gazed out. The sun had only recently set and the sky was still shot with crimson and orange. Gradually, as she stood there, it darkened until only a faint rosy glow remained. Across the water the lights of Craigmond twinkled out. A peaceful scene, yet a feeling of threat remained with her.

Shivering, but not from cold, Jayne drew the curtains and prepared herself for bed. Clad in a nightgown and peacock-blue robe, she was sitting at the dressing-table mirror brushing her hair when there was a knock on the door. "Who is it?" she called uneasily.

"It's me . . . Duncan. I want to talk to you, Jayne."

Her throat clenched, but she managed to stammer out, "Please . . . leave it until morning."

"No, it won't wait," he said insistently. "I must see you."

Jayne rose to her feet and went to stand by the door. The thought that he was so close made her shiver with excitement. "I told you, I'm tired," she said.

"It's a tiredness that came on very suddenly." There was an ominous impatience in his voice. "I think I'm entitled to an explanation, Jayne."

She was caught up in an agony of indecision. If she let him into her room, how could she hope to face him calmly and not betray the true state of her emotions? But if she refused, was she not making the situation even more obvious to him? There could only be one real reason for keeping him out . . . that she was afraid of the effect he would have on her.

With sudden decision she turned the key in the lock, and stood back. Duncan stepped inside and closed the door behind him.

"Well . . ." She faltered. "What is it you want?"

His eyes appraised her slowly, taking in every detail of her slender figure draped in the flowing peacock-blue satin. "You look fantastic!" he murmured from deep in his throat.

"I asked what you want," she pointed out, attempting, and failing miserably, to put an edge of steel to her voice.

Duncan's dark glance seemed to suggest that it was a stupid question. "I wanted to know why you ran out on me, Jayne."

"I didn't!" she protested. "I was tired, so I decided to come up to bed."

He frowned with quick irritation. "Quit acting . . . for once in your life! You could easily have waited downstairs a few minutes until I had finished on the phone. But you were afraid to face me, weren't you? Why, Jayne? What was it you were afraid of?"

She clenched her fists in desperation. "Why won't you believe what I tell you?"

"Why? Because you're not telling me the truth." The words were spoken mildly, and only his tautened jawline revealed his deep, underlying anger. "Perhaps you would prefer me to put it into words for you?"

"Put what into words?" she faltered.

"That you're dead scared—scared of yourself! You realized suddenly that the game you've been playing with me was getting out of hand, and you weren't ready for the consequences . . . not yet. There's a name men use to describe a woman like you, Jayne."

She flushed scarlet. "You . . . you're talking insulting nonsense."

"Am I? Do you deny that you were behaving just now like a woman who can't get enough of a man? You were throwing yourself at me, responding in double measure to every advance I made."

"That's the wildest exaggeration!" she protested. "My response to you was . . . was due to the wine we had with dinner. You gave me two glasses, you remember? And there was the effect of the music, and . . ."

Duncan gave a harsh bark of laughter. "You'll have to do better than that, Jayne. Last time, you claimed that you were having yourself a little sex fantasy, with me cast in the role of my brother. And you seemed quite surprised that I found the idea of that highly offensive. Now your excuse is that I plied you with too much alcohol. Well, I'll tell you this, my dear sister-in-law—you reacted to me the way you did because you're a sexy, hot-blooded woman. I would only have to lay a finger on you again, and you'd no more hold out against me than you've done each time before. So why not admit the truth about yourself and stop playing your nasty little games?"

Jayne moistened her dry lips with the tip of her tongue. "I suppose you feel proud of your own behavior?" she flung at him. "I suppose you think it's fine to take advantage of a woman when she's . . ." A sob caught in her throat. Fingering her rings, she faltered on weakly, ". . . when she's feeling bewildered and lost, and desperately needing the warmth of human contact to help find herself again."

"Well done!" exclaimed Duncan, clapping his hands mockingly. "Act two, scene three of—which play was that from?"

"I'm not acting!" she screamed.

His eyes glinted like jet stones. "Oh yes you are, Jayne. But I'll tell you when you *weren't* acting. Downstairs just now, and the other times I've kissed you. There was none of this pretended timidity then, no fake display of outraged modesty."

"I've tried to explain . . ." she began.

But Duncan ignored her as he continued, "That phone call from Fiona came in the nick of time for you, didn't it? You were well on the way to letting your natural instincts have free rein, but the interruption gave you time to cool down a bit and change your tactics."

"You couldn't be more wrong," she said chokingly. But how could she hope he would believe that, when in her own heart she knew it was a flagrant lie? Even now, at this very moment, her anger and bitterness against him were being swamped by a desperate longing to feel his arms about her once more.

"I couldn't be more *right,* you mean," Duncan drawled. "If not for that fortuitous phone call, you would by now be in no position to go on pretending. We'd have made love, Jayne, wild abandoned love, and you would still be panting for more. I can recognize a passionate woman when I hold one in my arms."

She tried to throw the sneer back into his face. "I suppose you've had plenty of experience?" she suggested bitingly.

"Enough." He jerked out that one brief word and said no more.

Jayne knew that he was still taunting her, but she couldn't help herself. "No doubt you find Fiona always ready and eager to oblige?" she flung out recklessly.

There was a long, throbbing pause, then Duncan inquired equably, "Are you jealous, Jayne?"

"Jealous?" She was horribly aware that her laugh had a ring of falsity. "Heavens, you do have an overrated opinion of yourself!"

"So my marriage to Fiona would have your blessing, would it?"

"You don't need my blessing," she countered, feeling a sick hollowness at the pit of her stomach.

"No, I don't *need* your blessing," he agreed. "I was merely inquiring as a matter of interest whether or not I would get it."

She lifted her shoulders. "If you must know, I'm completely indifferent on the subject of Fiona."

"I'm relieved to hear that." He smiled a cruel smile. "I don't expect you two women to be close buddies, but at least I'll be spared any nastiness when she comes over tomorrow."

Jayne felt cold dismay claw at her. "Fiona is . . . is coming here?"

"That's what she telephoned about. She suggested bringing her parents over for a couple of days. Sir Douglas is a keen fisherman, and of course we hope to get in some sailing, too." He paused a moment. "Do *you* sail, Jayne?"

"I . . . I don't think so."

"Fiona is very keen," he told her dryly. "And very expert, I might add."

Jayne held her head high, though in reality she felt like flopping into a chair and giving way to tears. "How nice for her."

"Isn't it?" He smiled.

The silence that fell between them was charged with tension. Jayne had to concentrate on forming words, as if speech was something that had to be mastered anew. When at last her voice emerged, it sounded strange and strangled to her own ears. "Will you please go now, Duncan? I'd like to get to bed."

"Alone?" he said ironically. "You want to spend the entire night tossing and turning in frustration? I have a much better idea."

She steeled herself to walk past him and hold the door open. "I asked you to go."

He nodded, as if acquiescing, and strode briskly toward her. But in the doorway he paused, and his gaze burned into her. "There's still time to change your mind, Jayne."

"No!" It was not the adamant refusal she had intended, but a groaning plea. She was begging him to end this torture. Standing there, he was much too close for her peace of mind.

Very slowly, Duncan raised his hand and touched her throat at a point just below the chin. With one finger he outlined the V of her robe in a feather-light caress on her bare skin. Then his hand came to a halt, hovering at the spot where the satin fabric folded across. Jayne felt a rush of arousal and her breasts tingled with a longing to be touched.

"If I do go," he murmured softly, "you'll regret it."

Jayne was spellbound, unable to think of anything but her need for him. The next instant she was locked in his arms, and his lips took possession of hers in a kiss of fierce intensity. Jayne clung to him with a kind of desperation, her arms locked around his neck, exulting in the pulsing heat of his desire.

With one smooth movement he lifted her off her feet and carried her to the bed, laying her none too gently on the downy satin quilt and flinging himself on top of her. As they kissed again Jayne drew him even closer, her hands roaming across his back. Her flimsy night attire offered no resistance to his own exploring hands, and she cared nothing that he was in a mood to tear the garments from her and leave her naked. . . .

Fiona . . . From nowhere the name snapped into Jayne's mind, and it jerked her to her senses. From being Duncan's eager and willing victim, she switched to fighting him off with frenzied strength. She clenched her fists into two hard balls and pummeled his chest, kicking with her feet and writhing beneath him. "Let me go!" she gasped. "Let me go!"

For a few moments longer he held her there, trapped on the bed, resisting her frantic struggles with contemptuous ease. But then, as if suddenly tiring of the game, he released her and got to his feet. He stood by the bed, glaring down at her furiously. Then he turned on his heel and strode out of the room, slamming the door behind him.

Chapter Seven

"I can't stay here on Kilraven now," said Jayne emphatically, taking her seat at the breakfast table.

"Why not?" queried Duncan, as though genuinely surprised.

"I should have thought," she retorted, "that it was perfectly obvious why not."

This was a confrontation Jayne would dearly have liked to avoid, but it seemed imperative to face him and make her intention clear without delay.

Duncan looked fresh and alert this morning, even more devastatingly handsome than usual, while she herself felt utterly drained. Just as he had forecast, she'd spent a long, sleepless night, tossing and turning wretchedly.

"You are my sister-in-law, and for the time being this is your home," he said, pouring cream into a bowl of porridge. "I see no good reason why you shouldn't remain here."

Jayne stared at him in amazement. It really was the limit the way he could meet her gaze with such calm assurance after what had happened in her room last night.

"Do you seriously mean, Duncan, that it wouldn't embarrass you to have me here while your fiancée and her parents come to stay?"

Instead of answering, he said blandly, "Do have some porridge, Jayne, it's very good. Er . . . you referred to my fiancée. I have always been under the impression that a man and woman are only engaged when an announcement has been made of the fact."

"You know what I mean," she snapped.

"I'm afraid I don't. In any case, if you were to leave Kilraven, where would you go?"

"I've already told you that. Sandy McFadden can fix me up with a job at the cottage hospital."

"And I've already told *you*—it's out of the question."

Her lower lip quivered as she regarded him across the table. "Can't you ever behave with normal decency? I'm asking nothing of you—nothing at all—except that you stop interfering in my life."

"I'm afraid your price is too high, Jayne!" He lifted the cover of a silver chafing dish. "Mmm! Grilled kippers. What could make a better start to the day? Can't I tempt you?"

Watching him dig in with a keen appetite, Jayne felt defeated. She had thought last night that she hated him, and in her mind she did. But her treacherous body responded to his nearness even now. She was fascinated by the economy of his movements as he dexterously boned the kippered herring, wielding knife and fork with consummate precision. It was difficult to equate him now with the man she had seen in a state of unbridled passion. . . .

She shivered, and tried to sip from her coffee cup without letting him see how her hand was trembling.

The McEwans were due to land on the island at four o'clock, after crossing the Sound in their motor launch. Fifteen minutes beforehand, Duncan set off in the car to meet them at the jetty. From a sense of defiance, Jayne herself set off a few moments later for a walk, taking Fyfe and Lady with her. She didn't intend to be waiting meekly at Kilraven House when the visitors arrived, and have them patronize her as a poor relation.

At the first cottage she came to, she received a friendly greeting from an old woman who sat knitting in the doorway. In the past few days, since Lady's accident, she had noticed a great change in the islanders' attitude toward her. What she had done for the injured red setter was regarded as something of a miracle, akin to the laying on of hands. Jayne now found herself treated with courtesy and respect, instead of cool hostility, wherever she went on Kilraven.

"Respect has to be earned," Duncan had told her, and it seemed that unwittingly she had achieved it.

Going forward, she bent to admire the old woman's handiwork, a fisherman's jersey in the intricate pattern that was unique to the Isle of Kilraven. "It's really beautiful," she said sincerely, fingering the thick, oily wool.

"Thank you, my lady." The compliment was accepted with simple pride. "Yon Miss McEwan is coming to visit at the House, I am hearing, and her father and mother, too?"

"Yes, that's right," Jayne confirmed. "Just for a few days."

The sharp old eyes were fixed on her face. "Is she to become the laird's lady, Mistress Stewart?"

"I . . . I don't really know." Jayne faltered and

wished now that she hadn't stopped to chat. "It's very probable, I should think."

"Aye." In that one simple word was locked away centuries of resignation to the inevitable.

As Jayne strolled on she found that she could take very little comfort from the fact that Fiona McEwan was disliked by the islanders. Fiona would not bother to seek their approval, would not even particularly want it. She'd consider them too far beneath her in the social scale to warrant anything but queenly condescension.

Lady's shoulder had caused her little trouble after the first couple of days, and she was scampering about now with almost her old zest. Even so, Jayne knew that it wasn't fair to prolong this excursion unduly, and after a while she reluctantly turned her footsteps back to the house.

There was no one about as she went in, and she guessed that everyone was upstairs dressing for dinner. Dreading the evening ahead of her, she too went up to her room. She drew herself a bath and lay soaking in the tub of piping hot water scented with sandalwood essence, while she pondered what to wear. There was really only one possibility, though, the lovely flowing, floating silk jersey gown in that glorious shade of red. Wearing that, there was a chance that Fiona McEwan wouldn't succeed in totally putting her in the shade.

When Jayne stepped into the dress fifteen minutes later and zipped it up, she had the strangest sensation of familiarity. She stood before the full-length wall mirror and gazed thoughtfully at her reflection. It was like looking at herself through a long, dark tunnel . . . in another time, another place. A man's voice was saying, faintly but yet as clear as the chime of a distant church bell on a calm summer day, "You look lovely in that dress, darling."

The image faded, and no more words echoed in her mind. But Jayne knew excitedly that this was the first *real* breakthrough of memory. The voice had obviously been her husband's, the caring voice of a man who truly loved her. This she had known in her heart all along, whatever other people might think about her and about Iain Stewart. She would never have married a man she didn't love, a man who didn't love her just as unreservedly in return.

As she slowly brushed her hair, making it gleam like finespun gold in the evening sunlight, she tried to recapture the experience of familiarity. She studied her reflection long and hard, but saw only the slender figure and moderately attractive features of the girl she had known herself to be for the few short days since she had woken up in the hospital.

Some minutes later, realizing with dismay how much time she had allowed to slip by, she left her room and hurried downstairs. The Great Hall was brightly lit from the five huge brass chandeliers. In the wide stone hearth was a fire of enormous pine logs, each the size of half a tree.

Jayne hurried on to the double doors of the large drawing room at the farther end. As she opened them and stood hesitantly in the doorway, the conversation ceased abruptly. In addition to Duncan and Fiona and an older couple who were quite clearly her parents, there was Duncan's factor, Robert MacLeod, and a rather stocky, pleasant-faced woman who Jayne guessed must be his wife.

Fiona was the first to speak. "My my, what an entrance!" she exclaimed, with a little tinkle of laughter. "It's such an advantage to have had stage training!"

"I'm sorry," Jayne said, with an apologetic glance at Duncan. "I didn't mean to be late, only . . ."

"Never mind, Jayne, you're here now." His look was

scathing as he strode briskly toward her and put a hand under her elbow. "Come and meet Sir Douglas and Lady McEwan. And this is Agnes MacLeod, Robert's wife."

Lady McEwan, a slim, silver-haired woman in an elegant gown of crimson silk, seemed a gentle person, the very antithesis of her daughter. She expressed her sympathy over the traumatic experience of the plane crash. Then Agnes MacLeod said brightly, "That was a fine thing you did for Lady the other day, Mrs. Stewart. The poor wee beastie was in dreadful pain, so the laird told my Robbie."

"What was that?" asked Sir Douglas interestedly. He was a tall, distinguished-looking man and, like Duncan and the factor, was attired in kilted evening wear, with a black velvet jacket and a lace jabot at the neck.

Duncan, pointing at Lady, who lay crouched on the hearth rug beside Fyfe, explained. "One of the dogs dislocated a shoulder the other day when she slipped and fell. We were some distance from home and she couldn't even bear me to touch her. I was wondering what on earth to do. Then Jayne arrived on the scene. I told her to run back to the house and have the vet sent for, but instead of obeying she pushed me aside and calmed Lady down while she investigated the injury. A moment later, with a little click, the joint was back in position. It was quite dramatic."

"Jayne has a keen sense of the dramatic," Fiona commented. "What a pity she ever left the stage when she so obviously has a talent for giving an impressive performance."

It was clear that Fiona's parents didn't hear the venom behind her remark. Nor did the MacLeods. Whatever Duncan might have thought, he concealed behind a smiling mask.

"Will you return to your stage career, Mrs. Stewart?" Lady McEwan inquired pleasantly. "I mean, of course, when you have recovered your memory."

This was a question that Jayne had already considered in her own mind, and she gave an honest answer. "I somehow can't visualize myself on the stage, Lady McEwan. The way I feel now, I'd be petrified of standing up before an audience."

"You underestimate yourself," Fiona drawled. "I imagine that acting, like riding a bicycle, is a trick that once learned is never forgotten. Even when one can't remember anything else," she added with a sneer.

"I hardly think, Fiona, that you can equate an art form with a simple physical skill like riding a bike," put in Duncan. "However, it's true that Jayne seems to have forgotten none of her 'professional' talents."

"Oh?" The monosyllable carried a wealth of suspicion.

Duncan didn't attempt to explain any further, but Jayne could read the mockery in his dark eyes as his gaze came to rest on her. She knew perfectly well what he was alluding to, and she felt her cheeks burn with color.

She was clearly the odd one out in this gathering, a fact that became even more apparent when the guests took their seats at the dinner table. There were three couples. Sir Douglas and Lady McEwan, Mr. and Mrs. MacLeod, Duncan and Fiona. And herself . . . a surplus woman.

Fiona seemed ruthlessly determined to steal the limelight away from Jayne and make herself the focus of attention. She began by holding forth on the subject of golf, at which she clearly regarded herself as an expert. "You know, Duncan," she mused, "you really should lay out a golf course here on Kilraven. Just a small nine-hole one, I mean."

"I've thought about it," he replied, "but each possi-

ble site would entail moving out several of the crofters."

"What's the problem?" she demanded. "You could
put them somewhere else, I imagine."

"True. But that's not quite the point, is it?"

Fiona shrugged impatiently. "What's the sense of
being laird if you don't take full advantage of the
privileges that go with it?"

Quite obviously, Jayne reflected, there would be
some big changes made when Fiona became the Laird
of Kilraven's lady. Consideration for the tenants' feelings wouldn't rank very high on her list of priorities.

"By the way, Duncan," she went on coaxingly, "are
you coming to watch me when I play in the ladies'
tournament at the R and A next month?"

Duncan translated for Jayne's benefit. "That's the
Royal and Ancient Golf Club at St. Andrews, near
Dundee. You probably know that it's recognized the
world over as the home of golf, and—"

"Well," Fiona interrupted crossly, "*are* you coming?"

"I'm not sure yet that I can get away," he told her.
"It's a busy time of year here on Kilraven."

"For heaven's sake, why keep a dog if you're going to
bark yourself?" At once she turned a smiling face to the
factor, as if to convey the fact that the words were not
meant rudely. But Jayne saw Robert MacLeod's face
flush with resentment.

"Fiona," her father reproved, "that remark was most
uncalled for."

Duncan broke in smoothly. "In a way, Sir Douglas,
Fiona has a point. With a supremely competent man
like Robbie supervising things for me, I could safely go
off and leave everything in his capable hands."

"The laird's place is here with his people," said
Robert soberly.

"We are in agreement about that," confirmed Duncan. He and Robert MacLeod exchanged smiles, and Jayne realized that the two men understood one another very well.

Fiona wisely decided to change the subject. She talked instead about what she intended to do while on Kilraven. "Do you ride horseback?" she asked Jayne.

"Yes, I do. At least, I believe I do."

"What's your swimming like?" was the next question.

Jayne considered a moment. "Fairly good, I think."

"Oh! What about sailing?"

"I don't think I've ever done any," she replied.

"Too bad! I want to get in as much sailing as I possibly can. I adore it. And of course Duncan handles a boat superbly."

After dinner, back in the elegant, silk-curtained drawing room, someone suggested cards and the four older people settled to a rubber of bridge. Fiona wandered over to the grand piano, raised the lid, and ran her hands lightly up and down the keyboard.

"Do *you* play, Jayne?" she inquired languidly.

Though instinctively Jayne felt that she did, whether she could reach Fiona's standard was another matter. However, she answered in a brisk, confident voice, "As a matter of fact, that's something else I'm sure I can do."

The piano lid was closed with a bang. Jayne felt Duncan's gaze upon her and glanced up in time to see his expression of amusement. She had a sudden fear that he would try to humiliate her by asking her to play something.

Fiona had drawn aside one of the long brocade drapes. She said, "It's a really perfect evening. What about a stroll, Duncan, while the others are playing cards?"

"If you like. Jayne, will you come?"

"No, thank you." She hadn't the slightest wish to spend a minute longer in Fiona's company than she was obliged to.

Duncan hesitated. "Sure?"

"Oh, for heaven's sake, come on," Fiona said irritably. "The girl said no, didn't she?"

"Won't you want a wrap?" he asked her.

Fiona uttered a soft laugh, full of meaning. "I doubt if I shall suffer from the cold, do you?"

They left by way of the french windows, which opened onto a terrace. Jayne had imagined herself glad to see them go, but she was suddenly seized with a jealousy so intense that she felt dizzy. What were Duncan and Fiona doing out there in the fragrant summer night? Was he holding Fiona in his arms as he had held *her?* She clenched her hands together in a fever of misery. She felt a sickening pain in the region of her heart that spread until it gripped her entire body. Her legs suddenly felt weak and trembling, and she stumbled to the nearest chair and sank into it.

"Are you all right, dear?" asked a voice from close by. Jayne opened her eyes and focused with difficulty on the anxious, homely face of Agnes MacLeod. "You're looking so pale," the older woman murmured. "Can I get you something? A wee nip of brandy?"

Jayne summoned a tremulous smile. "Thank you, no. I . . . er, I think I must have had too much wine at dinner. If you don't mind, I think I'd like to go up to bed."

"Yes, my dear, of course. I'm sure you're wise to get plenty of rest at this difficult time. I'll explain to the laird."

Upstairs in her bedroom, Jayne paced the carpet, far too restless for bed. The thought suddenly struck her that the windows of this room overlooked the terrace.

Crushing down her qualms about eavesdropping, she put out the lights, then drew back the curtains of one window. Very carefully, so as not to make a betraying sound, she eased open the casement.

Fiona's voice floated up to her, low-pitched yet so distinct that Jayne knew she and Duncan must be standing directly below. "Aren't you getting a little bit weary, darling, of the lost-memory act that Jayne has been putting on?"

"What makes you so sure it's an act?" he countered.

"Heavens, isn't it obvious? You men are so easily duped when it comes to scheming women."

Duncan protested mildly. "Oh, I don't know about that."

"It's true! Consider all the things you know about her, and the disgraceful way she behaved toward you when Iain died, and yet you're still fool enough to have her stay here. I don't know why you don't just send her packing."

"She *is* my sister-in-law," he pointed out.

"But you'd never even met the girl until she landed herself on you, virtually destitute . . . just cabling first that she was on her way. What would you have done, I wonder, if the plane *hadn't* crashed? Would you still have welcomed her with open arms?"

"Must we go on talking about Jayne?" he asked.

A lengthy silence ensued. Though Jayne strained her ears, she could hear nothing. Then from Fiona came the soft, excited laugh of a woman who has been most thoroughly and expertly kissed.

"I rather think we'd better go inside now." This was Duncan.

"Must we?" asked Fiona, with a reluctant sigh.

"Yes," he said firmly. "I mustn't be discourteous to my guests."

There was another silence, followed by another

gurgle of laughter from Fiona. Then Jayne heard the French windows being opened as the two of them went inside.

Clad warmly against the early morning chill, Jayne climbed an upward path through a grove of silver birch trees to a point which overlooked the rocky moorland pastures and the glittering blue expanse of the sea. Despite her unhappiness, her heart lifted at the sheer beauty of the scene. The air was filled with all the lovely fragrances of early summer, and there was a sweetness in the sound of the wind, which caressed her cheeks and fanned out her honey-gold hair.

She had been rather surprised when, slipping out through the silent house, the two dogs had failed to come running. The reason for this was explained when they suddenly appeared now, bounding up to her joyfully and prancing around her with excited little yelps. A minute later, their master came into view from behind a shoulder of rock.

"Good morning, Jayne!" he called. "I trust you slept well?"

"No, I didn't," she replied candidly, before she could stop herself.

"Pity! Did you have something on your mind to keep you awake?" Duncan's face revealed nothing but friendly inquiry, but she could detect the mockery behind his voice.

"Perhaps I went to bed too early," she said. "Before I was properly tired, I mean."

"Could be. It was certainly a surprise when Fiona and I returned to the drawing room to find that you had already gone up."

"Hardly a disappointment, though."

"Why do you say that?" he inquired blandly.

Jayne shrugged. "Fiona would like to see me gone

away altogether; she made that very plain. So why don't you tell her that I *want* to go, that I'm longing to get away, only you won't let me?"

"I can't prevent you going, Jayne."

"You can stop me taking that job at the hospital, and in the circumstances that amounts to the same thing."

"The most sensible course for you to adopt," he said patiently, as if talking to an unreasonable child, "is to remain here until such time as your memory returns. You know that very well, Jayne."

She sighed unhappily. "Are you sure you don't agree with Fiona that I'm a scheming woman who's putting on a big act?"

Duncan's smile broadened, and derision danced in his black eyes. "We have a Scots proverb to this effect: *Listen at a hole, and ye'll hear news o' yoursel'.* Rather apt, don't you think? Or as you Sassenachs would put it, *Listeners seldom hear good of themselves.*"

Jayne stared at him in horror. "You . . . you *knew!*"

"That you were eavesdropping from your window? Yes, I knew."

"In that case," she said, anger thrusting through her acute embarrassment, "you might have had the decency not to go on talking about me like that."

"Since you've introduced the subject of decency," Duncan countered, "do you consider it *decent* to deliberately go out of your way to listen to a private conversation? What were you hoping to overhear, Jayne, when you opened your window? A few passionate groans and grunts, perhaps?"

"That's a despicable thing to suggest," she said, turning away from him. But fingers of steel clamped on her arm and jerked her back to face him.

"It ill becomes you, my dear sister-in-law, to accuse *me* of despicable behavior. Look to your own past record."

"What's that supposed to mean?"

"Oh, I forgot. You don't remember, *do you?*" The doubt was back in his voice, as if he was wondering afresh if she was only pretending to suffer from amnesia. "Well, when your memory *does* come back, let's hope you'll have the grace to feel a modicum of shame."

"Tell me what I'm supposed to have done," Jayne demanded, trying in vain to wrench her arm from his bruising grip.

"It would make no sense to you, if you can't remember," he stated, and added as if to himself, "It made no sense to me."

"If I did something unforgivably wrong, then tell me." She laid her free hand on his arm beseechingly. "Please, Duncan."

His jaw went taut. For an instant he stared down at her, his black eyes blazing. Then in a sudden swift movement Jayne was enveloped in his arms. "Is it deliberate?" he muttered thickly against her hair. "Or does it just come naturally to you?"

"I don't know what you're talking about," she cried.

Desperately, she struggled to free herself, only to find that with each movement her body was brought into closer and more intimate contact with his virile frame. As always when Duncan held her in his arms, there was no real tenderness, no sincere caring, just sheer brute passion. Yet even so, with all the bitterness and hatred between them, his urgent desire awoke deep longings within her, her innate feminine instincts answering the call of the male hunter.

"Please," she sobbed, "let me go!"

Duncan held her back from him so that he could look into her face. His eyes were dark unfathomable pools in which, as so often before, she longed to drown herself.

"You use every trick in the book against me," he

said, gritting his teeth. "Then you calmly expect me to let you go. But it's a dangerous game you play, Jayne. You've made me crazy to possess your lovely body, and by heaven I mean to have it! So why not right here and now? Where better than a fragrant bed of heather under the canopy of the summer sky?"

The thought of surrendering to his lovemaking was infinitely sweet, infinitely tempting. If only there had been the tiniest spark of love for her in Duncan's stony heart, the tiniest shred of tenderness! She wouldn't hold back then. No, she would give herself to him freely, gladly, with joyful abandon, heedless of any thought about right or wrong . . . if only Duncan cared. But she knew despairingly that he cared not one jot for her.

She made one last plea. "Let me go, Duncan," she begged. "Let me leave Kilraven. I don't just mean across the water to Craigmond, but to go away from the district altogether. I could leave at once, today, and we need not see one another ever again."

Duncan was breathing deeply, jerkily, as he fought for self-control. His voice was husky with unfulfilled desire. "You'll not leave this island, Jayne, until I say you may."

A surge of defiance made her flare. "You can't prevent me if I want to go."

"You will not go!" Was it an order, or a confident prediction? But what did it matter? Either way, Jayne knew that she didn't have the strength to leave Kilraven of her own free will. Was it the spell of this enchanted island, or the spell of this devastatingly attractive man? But the two were indivisible. *I am Kilraven, and Kilraven is me!*

Unbidden tears welled up behind her lids, and a few broke free to tumble down her cheek. Still held trapped in Duncan's arms, she could not prevent him from noticing.

"Tears now!" He gave a short bark of laughter. "I suppose you've been trained to weep to order? But you won't melt my heart as easily as that, sister-in-law, because I know you for what you are."

Jayne felt suddenly cold, bereft, as his arms dropped away. He turned and called to the dogs, who came to heel at once. When he swung back to her, his face was a smiling mask.

"A brisk early morning walk is just the thing to give one an appetite, so I won't keep you, Jayne. See you at breakfast, no doubt."

With a brief nod, he strode off briskly through the heather. The two setters, their tongues lolling from panting mouths, looked up at Jayne expectantly. But when she didn't make a move, they turned away and bounded after the man who was their lord and master.

By midmorning Jayne once again felt painfully aware of being a surplus woman when the MacLeods came to call for Sir Douglas and Lady McEwan. Robbie had promised the previous evening to show Sir Douglas the best trout stream on the island, while Agnes was taking Lady McEwan to see some of the crofters' weaving. Duncan, it seemed, when he took over as laird, had enlisted the aid of his factor's wife to encourage the art of home weaving on Kilraven. Now, four years later, it was a thriving cottage industry. The cloth produced, which rivaled the famous tweed of Harris Island, found a ready market in exclusive shops in London and New York.

Duncan and Fiona had set out for a sail a half hour earlier—at Fiona's urgent insistence. As a matter of politeness, Duncan had asked Jayne if she would like to join them. He hadn't pressed the point, though, when she declined the invitation, merely commenting that perhaps it was just as well, since the water was rather choppy for a novice sailor.

From the window of her bedroom, Jayne was watching the two of them now. She was using a pair of powerful binoculars, which normally hung from a hook in the portico, and they brought the boat startlingly near.

It was only too apparent that Fiona was perfectly at home crewing for Duncan, expertly leaning out over the water to lend her weight when necessary, and ducking neatly for the boom to swing over her each time he pulled the tiller across to change tack. On one such occasion she used Duncan's knee as a lever to haul herself upright again, and Jayne noticed the way she smiled up at him provocatively.

Later everyone assembled for lunch, using the small dining room this time. Sir Douglas boasted amiably about his morning's catch, while his wife talked eagerly about her outing with Agnes. "Wherever we went, your praises were being sung, Duncan," she told him. "The women all say what a wonderful extra source of income the weaving is, especially when it's a bad year for crops or fishing."

"And it must be a profitable line for you, too, Duncan," put in Fiona.

He raised an inquiring eyebrow at her. "I don't follow you."

"Well, it stands to reason that a quality product like Kilraven tweed must carry a good profit margin on your marketing operation. What do you reckon to clear? Twenty-five percent, or more?"

"I make no profit," he said tersely. "It's a small service I can do for my tenants, and I do it gladly."

Fiona shook her head in smiling disapproval. "You

really will have to learn something about business practice, my sweet!"

"Now, now, Fiona," said her father with a frown. "Having failed so completely in your own business venture, you're hardly in a position to be critical of Duncan. In any case—and I speak at first hand as one who has been financially involved with him—the Laird of Kilraven needs no instruction in business acumen."

The angry glance that Fiona directed at her father made her lovely face look twisted and ugly for a moment. "I was merely pointing out," she said, with a dismissive shrug, "that for Duncan not to take his fair percentage will be interpreted as weakness. It's simply a matter of letting these people know who's boss."

Jayne glanced covertly at Duncan, who was seated at the head of the table, and saw a little, hooded smile. *If Fiona seriously imagined for one moment,* she thought shiveringly, *that Duncan was anything less than absolute master on Kilraven, she understood nothing.* He was so much the master, the laird, that far from being taken as a sign of weakness, his generosity to the crofters was repaid tenfold with the sort of loyalty and respect that could be witnessed on every side.

Conversation turned to the afternoon's activities. The two older people opted for a quiet nap in a sunny spot on the terrace, and Duncan suggested that he and the two girls should go riding. Fiona pouted and insisted that she would rather sail again, but Duncan wouldn't be moved.

"This time we'll do something that Jayne can join in," he said firmly.

Fiona gave her a sharp look. "I don't expect she'd enjoy riding any more than sailing. It's one thing for her to *think* that she can handle a horse, and quite another to actually do it."

Feeling strangely confident, Jayne shrugged off the sneer and said quietly, "I'd like to try, anyway. I can only fall off, can't I?"

It seemed to her that Duncan's expression held a modicum of respect. "I'll give Fergus a ring and ask him to fix you up with two ponies," he said.

"Nothing too docile for me," put in Fiona quickly. "I don't want a mount without any spirit."

"You'll have to take what you get," said Duncan, softening his rebuke by the mildness of his tone. "Apart from my Tristram, there are no horses kept on Kilraven merely for pleasure riding."

They went off to get changed and Jayne put on a pair of jeans and a thick sweater. She waited downstairs for several minutes before Fiona made an appearance. To Jayne's chagrin, she looked exquisite in tan boots, cavalry twill jodhpurs, and an expertly tailored black velvet jacket. Her red-gold hair had been swept up under a hard riding hat.

Duncan came striding in from outside, and Jayne was gladdened on two counts: first, that he too wore jeans, together with a gray sweatshirt, and second, that he had thoughtfully brought a hard hat for her, which fit perfectly when she tried it on.

The two ponies, Muffin and Kelpie, were awaiting them in the stable yard. Both fox-colored, with flowing silver manes and tails, they stood quietly together eyeing Duncan's proud black stallion, Tristram.

"Oh, what beauties!" said Jayne, and went forward impulsively to stroke the soft velvet muzzles and fine, muscular necks. The mares' bright, kindly eyes blinked with contentment. "They're the Highland breed, aren't they?" she asked Duncan.

He nodded. "That's right, Jayne. On the mainland

they come a bit bigger, but these make the ideal general purpose pony for this sort of country."

"Very surefooted, I imagine?"

"Oh, very. They offer a comfortable ride, too, at their natural pace . . . walking or trotting. They're a bit rougher at the gallop, but then we won't be trying that."

Fiona, arbitrarily making her choice without any reference to Jayne, had already swung expertly into Muffin's saddle. "Can't we get on," she demanded impatiently, "instead of wasting half the afternoon talking? The ponies are here to be ridden, not admired."

As Jayne prepared to mount, Duncan came forward to give her a leg up. But then he paused, watching interestedly as she stood correctly with her back to the pony's head, placed her left foot well home in the stirrup, and sprang with one smooth movement into the saddle. She had the satisfaction of seeing a sour look of disappointment on Fiona's face and knew that the other girl had been hoping she would make a mess of the operation.

They set off three abreast, Duncan in the middle. Cresting the central ridge of Beinn Liath Bheag, they were struck by a westerly breeze that was brisk and invigorating, carrying the sharp salt tang of the Atlantic Ocean. Below them was spread a lovely tapestry of color. Beyond the curving chain of silver-sand beaches, the surface of the sea was an astonishing grape blue, rippled and veined with glints of turquoise. The nearer Hebridean islands, seeming incredibly close in this magically clear atmosphere, were a rich, deep mossy green. In the pastures through which they descended— the *machair* as she had learned to call the meadowland here—the golden brightness of buttercups was giving way to the vivid blue of speedwell.

"In another week the yellow will have faded completely and the whole area will be one vast, shimmering sheet of blue," Duncan told them.

Jayne gazed around her. "It's so incredibly lovely. I just can't imagine a more beautiful place on earth."

Fiona had been silent. Now she suddenly spurred her pony into a gallop, calling gaily over her shoulder, "Come on, I'll race you to that standing stone over there."

Duncan shouted to her to come back, but she ignored him. Hastily telling Jayne, "Stay where you are!" he was off in pursuit of Fiona, his huge black stallion gaining on her with every stride.

Jayne paused for only a moment. She had no doubt of her ability to handle this sweet-natured little mare, and if Fiona was intent on making her look incompetent, she had a surprise in store. "Come on, Kelpie!" she said coaxingly.

The little mare responded at once, and they sped like the wind across the rolling, flower-embroidered meadowland. Ahead of them, Fiona's pony had slowed and was picking its way gingerly across the rocky bed of a stream. Duncan, having caught up with her now, took the water in an easy leap, then reined in abruptly to confront Fiona and prevent her from resuming the gallop.

Jayne herself raced on, delighting in the thrill of moving at such speed, in perfect harmony with her mount. Reaching the stream she didn't even hesitate, and neither did little Kelpie. Together they took the leap as cleanly and effortlessly as Duncan had done, then she too reined in and stopped. Flushed with triumph, she turned a laughing face to her companions. But to her utter dismay, Duncan's face seemed to be looming with thunder.

"I distinctly told you to stay where you were," he rasped. "What the devil did you think you were up to, galloping after us like that?"

"But I enjoyed it," she protested. "It was fun."

"Is a broken neck your idea of fun? You're no novice, Jayne, I grant you, but it was sheer madness to take that leap."

"I knew what I was doing," she said woodenly.

"You mean you *thought* you did! Just because you feel at home on a pony's back doesn't automatically indicate that you're an expert steeplechaser. Besides which, you're unfamiliar with both the pony and the terrain."

"I'm sorry," she muttered with ill grace.

"So I should hope!" he rejoined. "It was foolish of Fiona to break into a gallop, but after all, she's had a lot of experience riding in this sort of country. And at least she had the sense not to jump the stream."

"*You* jumped it," Jayne murmured, still defiant.

"Are you making comparisons?" he asked sarcastically. "Do you imagine that if *I* can do something, then so can you?"

"I didn't mean that," she said uncomfortably.

Fiona had been following this unpleasant exchange with a smug smile, and she couldn't resist putting her oar in. "However many hacks you may have ridden," she said nastily, "Duncan has had a hundred times your experience with horses. He came in first last month in the cross-country races at Achnadonnell."

They resumed their ride, but all the pleasure was gone for Jayne. Dropping behind, she watched Duncan and Fiona as they chatted and laughed together. A couple of times she saw Fiona stretch out a hand and touch Duncan's arm in a playful, chiding gesture.

Duncan made no attempt to urge Jayne to rejoin them, nor did he turn around to include her in their conversation. If you want to sulk, he seemed to be telling her, go ahead and sulk. It doesn't bother me in the least.

They were out for another hour before, to Jayne's intense relief, they at last clattered back into the stable yard.

Chapter Eight

At the window of her bedroom, where she had retreated before dinner, Jayne stood watching the flight of a golden eagle. In the cloud-dappled sky it soared and circled on silent wings, skillfully making use of the upward thermal currents. She felt envious of the great majestic bird for its glorious freedom.

Ever since returning from the ride she had been vacillating about what to do. A dozen times she had made a firm decision—and just as often she had reversed it. The sensible thing was to go right away from here, back to London where she might be able to pick up a few threads of her former life. To remain on Kilraven was an agony, and it was made doubly painful by Fiona's presence. Why should she suffer, Jayne asked herself, merely for the sake of Duncan's pride?

You will not go, he had commanded her. *You will not leave this island, Jayne, until I say you may.* His words beat at her brain, making her seethe with fury. What it

138

amounted to was that the Laird of Kilraven must not be seen to spurn his brother's widow. So she was expected to remain here on the island as his unwilling and unwelcome guest. On no account must she take a comparatively humble job as receptionist at the local cottage hospital. Duncan didn't care two straws about her feelings—just so long as she played the game according to *his* rules.

Well, she was darned if she would submit to his autocratic dictates!

But each time she had talked herself into defying Duncan, she was stabbed through by the humiliating knowledge that she could not bring herself to break this tenuous closeness with the man she loved, loved despite all the pain and heartache it entailed.

At length she turned away from the window and went to draw a bath. The unaccustomed exercise had produced a few minor aches, and it was pleasurable to lie soaking in a deep tub of steaming water, perfumed with sandalwood essence.

One ache that was deep within her, though, would never be soaked away: the ache to feel Duncan's arms about her again, to feel once more the possessive claim of his lips on hers. There was only one way to behave toward him from now on; she must be coolly and courteously aloof. And that must be her attitude to Fiona, too. If, as was only too likely, their engagement was announced during her present stay on Kilraven, Jayne was determined to be ready with polite congratulations and not betray any sign of her jealousy and anguish.

As there would only be the house party at dinner this evening, she chose a cocktail-hour sort of dress in a soft russet-brown silky fabric that clung to her slender figure. Yet downstairs, when she saw Fiona and her mother in long gowns, she felt gauche and out of place.

"Did you enjoy your ride this afternoon, my dear?" asked Sir Douglas as she entered the drawing room.

Jayne knew it was merely a casual question, yet somehow she felt under fire, conscious that Duncan and Fiona were watching her. "Yes, thank you," she said brightly.

"Isn't it interesting that you can ride so well, considering the sort of life you led . . . ?" Coloring at his tactlessness, he added, "In London, I mean. It's not exactly riding country, is it?"

"Oh, but I spent my childhood in the country."

Duncan demanded, "What makes you say that, Jayne?"

"I . . . I don't know, really. It just sort of came out."

"Can you remember any details?"

She thought for a few moments. "Absolutely nothing, I'm afraid. It's just an impression."

"A simple little country girl!" interjected Fiona. "But the image hardly fits, does it, with the life you've been leading? A bit-part actress, and . . . and everything!"

This was intended to be offensive, but Fiona's words were coated with sugar and her parents seemed to notice nothing amiss. Jayne felt certain that Duncan did, though. There was a curious expression in the depths of those ebony-black eyes, as if he found his sister-in-law something of an enigma.

Jayne met Fiona's gaze defiantly, refusing to be put down. "Surely it's no more odd than the fact that you—a sophisticated city girl, if ever there was one—should now have come to live in a remote part of Western Scotland."

Fiona lifted her slender shoulders. "You can hardly equate our two cases."

"I wouldn't want to," said Jayne sweetly. It gave her

a throb of satisfaction to see that her barb had found its mark.

After dinner Jayne sat it out in the drawing room for as long as she could bear. In the end, though, she feebly muttered an excuse about feeling tired, and said good night.

As she crossed the Great Hall she heard footsteps behind her, and before she had reached the head of the stairs Duncan had caught up with her.

"Jayne, just a moment!"

She stopped and turned to face him, her heart pounding. He stood on the stair below her, but he was still taller by a couple of inches. In the subdued light of a wall sconce, his lean face was deeply etched with shadows, but she could see the angry glitter in his eyes. "You're a fool to try and cross swords with Fiona," he rasped. "It's a game you can't hope to win."

"Win?" she echoed, somehow forcing a casual indifference into her voice. "What do you imagine that I'm trying to win?"

"Now you're attempting to be smart with me!" he snapped. "Pertness doesn't suit you, Jayne. It's not your style."

"That sounds suspiciously close to being a compliment," she said with a shaky laugh. "You'd better watch it, Duncan, or you might find yourself actually saying something nice to me. But that would never do, would it?"

He responded with a bitter look. "You little fool! Do you imagine that I wouldn't *like* to think well of you? If only I could!"

"What's to prevent you?" she asked, bewildered. "What am I doing that's so dreadful?"

"It's not so much what you're doing now," he countered, "as what you've done in the past."

Jayne gripped the massive carved banister rail until her knuckles gleamed palely white. "Isn't it time you told me what my offense was?" she flung at him. "Okay, I dared to marry your brother . . . a woman you didn't consider good enough for him. But that's hardly a crime, is it? It's the sort of thing that happens all the time, families not approving of the girl a man marries. But Iain was an adult, entitled to make up his own mind in choosing a wife. And it isn't even as if I enticed him away from Kilraven. He'd already left when we met, so you can't put the blame for that on me."

"Quite a speech!" drawled Duncan.

"So how about giving me some answers?"

His dark eyes lingered on her in a long, searching look. "It will be time enough to learn of your offense when your memory returns," he muttered at last.

Jayne shivered inwardly, but stuck to her guns. "If you would only talk about it all, it might help me recover my lost memory."

"There are some things it's best not to bring out into the open," he said, shaking his head. "In this case, it could only lead to more bitterness, more antagonism than ever."

"So instead you prefer to keep dropping these sinister hints," she cried passionately. "As if I'm some sort of untouchable."

"No, Jayne!" Duncan's voice was husky and deep in his throat. "That's been the whole cause of the trouble —the fact that you are infinitely touchable, infinitely desirable. . . ."

"Don't speak like that," she stormed. "It's humiliating."

"Why humiliating?" he demanded. "It's pure instinct with you, I suppose, to make yourself desirable to men, as natural a thing to you as eating and drinking. You've got Sandy McFadden dangling on a piece of string. And as for me . . ."

Jayne went very still, her throat suddenly dry and tight. When Duncan took a step up to the same stair on which she was standing, she shrank back from him, pressing herself against the banister. His nearness was almost overwhelming. She felt threatened by him—and just as much threatened by her own intense longing.

"As for me, Jayne," he went on at last, breaking the long, throbbing silence between them, "you know only too well, only too intimately, the effect you have on me."

She gave a little shiver, remembering. Each beat of her heart sent quivers of desire racing through her, and she had to fight a treacherous impulse to let her body melt against his, to twine her arms about his neck and draw his face down to hers in a long kiss. . . .

"I . . . I don't set out to make you want me," she murmured in a breathless whisper.

"Yet, you're at it now, this very moment—you're reaching out with those devilish, invisible tentacles and enmeshing me helplessly."

"I'm not doing anything of the kind," she protested hotly. "You can't make out that I'm in any way at fault. I was going up to my room, and you came chasing after me and stopped me."

"But you've made maximum use of the situation," he accused her.

"That's ridiculous," she retorted. "I'm just standing here talking to you—against my will! I'd much rather go on upstairs. I'm very tired."

"I thought you wanted some answers from me," he reminded her.

"Oh . . . yes, I do."

"In any case," he said, his gaze intent and compelling, "I doubt if you *could* break away from me at this moment."

Unfortunately, this was only too true. Jayne wished desperately that she could break free from his curious spell, that she could turn from him and mount the last few stairs, then walk steadily across the upper hall and along the corridor to her bedroom. But it was an impossibility. . . .

"Why do you talk in that ridiculous way?" She faltered. "Why do you keep on at me all the time? Isn't having Fiona available enough for you?"

"We'll leave Fiona out of this," he snapped.

"How can we leave her out? She's the girl you're going to marry."

He hesitated a moment, then said slowly, "You sound jealous, Jayne."

"Jealous?" Her show of scorn was miserably unconvincing. "Fiona is welcome to you, as far as I'm concerned! You and she are ideally suited to one another—two arrogant, overbearing people who seem to imagine that they're in a class apart and altogether superior to other human beings."

Whatever she might have gone on to say was abruptly cut short when Duncan reached out and swiftly pulled her to him, crushing her body against his. As his lips claimed hers in a harsh kiss, she felt herself dragged down into a spinning vortex of passion from which there was no escape . . . down, down, down, conscious only of their two bodies melding into one, of his cruel, roaming, kneading hands and hard demanding lips, of his heart thudding against her own. There seemed to be a clamorous tumult all around, deafening her ears; a searing red brilliance of light that blinded her vision.

And yet, above the clamor, she heard a voice calling, "Duncan, where are you?"

Fiona! A violent shock wave blasted through Jayne's body. Awareness and common sense came flooding back and she struggled to be free of Duncan's enveloping arms. He released her suddenly, shrugging his black velvet evening jacket into place. Jayne clutched at the banister, feeling that her unsteady legs would scarcely support her.

Duncan gave a soft, though shaky laugh, and murmured, "For one who's not the slightest bit jealous, my dear Jayne, you reacted most strangely to the sound of Fiona's voice." Then, immediately gaining command of himself, he called, "Just coming, Fiona! Be right with you!" He glanced at Jayne, and said softly, "Are you okay?"

"Yes!" she said fiercely. "Just go!"

Duncan lingered, looking at her doubtfully. From below Jayne heard quick footsteps rapping across the flagstones of the Great Hall.

"Please leave me!" she begged desperately, unable to face the scene she knew would arise if Fiona found them like this.

"Very well, if that's what you want."

For another split second he lingered, then turned and walked down the stairs, just in time to prevent Fiona's arrival. As though from very far off, Jayne could hear their voices.

"Where have you been?" Fiona asked peevishly. "You disappeared without a word and you've been gone ages, so I thought I'd come and find you, darling. I'm bored with watching TV, and I imagine that we could think of a better way to occupy our time, don't you?"

Sickened, Jayne heard Duncan's soft chuckle, which seemed to her to be charged with sensual implications. They walked off together, and Jayne visualized them clasped in a passionate embrace—just as she herself had been with Duncan only moments ago. She closed her eyes, trying to thrust the thought from her mind, but it refused to go.

With a heavy sigh, Jayne stirred herself and mounted the last three stairs to the upper hall. Her footsteps felt leaden, and it seemed an age before she reached the sanctuary of her bedroom. Once there, the door closed and locked behind her, she stood rigid and unmoving, her eyes dry, staring blindly into space. What a terrible curse had been laid upon her! Robbed of her memory, she was unable to feel grief for her dead husband and had fallen hopelessly in love with his brother, a man who despised her.

It drifted into her mind that Duncan had still not answered her question about why he felt such bitterness toward her. Did it really matter anymore? she wondered bleakly. But an insidious voice told her that she *must* find out. To remain in ignorance would be intolerable. Tomorrow, then, she would demand a proper interview with him—in his study! The businesslike atmosphere of that simply furnished room would not be conducive to sensual thoughts.

Again Jayne felt jealousy swamp her like a great tidal wave. She could not banish the hateful vision of Fiona and Duncan being together at this very moment, making love. It was an utterly humiliating thought, but right now she would give anything to be in Fiona's place.

Sometime in the small hours of the night, Jayne was startled from her restless dream. She tensed, ears alert. Within the house, everything was still and quiet; outside, only the ever-present sighing of the wind in the nearby trees and the distant murmur of breakers on the shore impinged upon the silence. Then, again, came the sound that had roused her, a soft rapping on the panel of her door.

"Who is it?" she called.

"It's me, Duncan."

She slid her feet to the floor and drew on her robe. Going across to the door, she asked in a low voice, "What is it you want now?"

"Let me in, Jayne."

"Of course not," she said indignantly. "It must be terribly late."

"It's two-thirty A.M., to be precise. Hurry up and let me in."

"Don't be absurd," she whispered. "What on earth are you thinking of?"

"We were interrupted before," he explained, "and there are things you should be made aware of, Jayne."

So Duncan had remembered her demand to know what it was she had done in the past to justify his contemptuous attitude toward her. But at this time of night! "I've waited for so long," she protested, "that I can wait now until morning. Go away!"

She heard him catch his breath in irritation. "This is vital, Jayne. If you don't let me in, I'll have to go and fetch Callum Blair's master key. Which is it to be?"

For a few brief moments she agonized. Wouldn't it be madness to admit Duncan to her bedroom and risk a repetition of the scene on the stairs? And yet, to refuse and have him force an entry with the master key would only make him angry—and that much less amenable to reason.

"I'm waiting, Jayne," he said warningly.

"Oh, very well."

When she turned the key and opened the door, Duncan strode in swiftly and closed it behind him. He was still kilted, but no longer wearing a jacket, and his shirt was unbuttoned at the neck. Jayne drew back from him, alarmed now that he was in her room, feeling instantly overpowered by his dominating presence.

"I couldn't settle to bed," he told her. "I knew that I'd never sleep."

"I've been awake too," she said, without considering the wisdom of such an admission.

"Have you, Jayne?" he queried. "Why was that, I wonder?"

She lifted her shoulders in a casual shrug. "Oh, I just felt a bit restless."

"But *why?* What made you restless?"

She grasped at a plausible reason. "I've been thinking and thinking about why you should have such a low opinion of me," she said tremulously. "When somebody thinks the worst of you . . ."

"But it doesn't *have* to be that way, Jayne," he broke in. "All we need is a little honesty between us."

"I . . . I don't know what you mean," she stammered.

Duncan raked a hand through his tousled hair in a restless gesture. "It's simple enough. Okay, we'll accept that you've lost your memory. But even so, you must recognize yourself for the sort of woman you are. So why not admit it? Why all this silly pretense?"

"What am I supposed to be pretending?" she asked faintly.

There was a look of scorn on his handsome face. "You want me, Jayne, just as much as I want you. You can't possibly deny it. Your body comes thrillingly alive the instant I lay a finger on you. Strange, isn't it, with a man you consider to be utterly despicable?"

Jayne struggled to summon up words of protest, but none came.

"The same question could be asked of me," he went on remorselessly. "Why do you fill me with tormenting desire, when I know all that I do know about you? There's a very simple answer, Jayne . . . it's purely a matter of chemistry."

"No!" she cried wretchedly.

"Yes! Everything between us is magnificently right, and our lovemaking would be something quite out of this world. You know it, and I know it."

"*Love*making," Jayne echoed contemptuously.

"You prefer to describe it as plain and simple sex?" he inquired, his black eyes stabbing into her. "Very well then, if you wish. It amounts to the same thing in the end."

"How can you suggest that?" she raged. "What kind of man are you, to be able to speak of lovemaking and mere loveless sex in the same breath?"

His gaze was unwavering, challenging her. "And what kind of woman are you, Jayne, to deny the urgent call of your instincts? I say that you are a deeply sensual woman who has at last found a man to whom every cell in her body is attuned. It wouldn't make one iota of difference if you and I were bitter enemies and had the fiercest hatred in the world for one another."

"You're wrong!" she sobbed. "You're totally, horribly wrong."

"Then how do you explain your electric reaction to me?" he asked, triumph in his voice.

"It's because I . . ." Jayne checked herself, appalled. How could she admit to Duncan that she was in love with him? He would only despise her all the more. Or he would insist that she was trying to put a glossy veneer on an emotion that was nothing higher than a physical lust to match his own.

He waited for her to answer, eyebrows quirked in mockery. At length Jayne muttered jerkily, "I've already told you, this strange position I'm in at the moment makes me extremely vulnerable. Is it so remarkable that I should clutch at anything that appears in the guise of tenderness, and—"

"So we're back to that interesting theory!" Duncan crossed his arms slowly, as if with weary impatience. "Can't you think of anything more original?"

"But it's true!" she insisted, hating herself because she was lying through her teeth. No other man on earth could have made her respond with such wild abandonment.

"Quit playing games," he muttered. "Can't you see what you're doing to me, Jayne?"

His tone had suddenly changed. It carried a warning note. Yet a need to wound him made her reckless. "Why not go to Fiona if you feel the need to assuage your sexual appetite?" she jibed. "I'm quite sure she would be only too ready to oblige you."

Duncan moved so swiftly that she was taken by surprise. His fingers dug cruelly into her shoulders. "We'll leave Fiona out of this," he snarled.

"Why should we, when she's—"

"I said leave her out of it! This is between you and me, Jayne, and no one else."

His grip on her shoulders seemed painful no longer. She found herself exulting in the fierce, possessive pressure of his fingers and longed for an even closer contact. She longed for him to lock his arms about her, yearned for him to kiss her. Every instinct to resist had fled before his potent magnetism, yet a tiny shred of sanity still remained in the recesses of her mind.

"Let me go!" he cried feebly.

Unexpectedly, Duncan eased his harsh grip on her shoulders. But the next instant she was enveloped in his arms in an embrace that was strangely tender. Instantly she felt a warm flood of love for him. Though acutely aware of the danger of allowing herself to respond, she could not help herself. She slid her flat palms up over the muscled contours of his chest and twined her arms about his neck, pressing her soft flesh against him to feel the burning fever-heat of his body, the primitive thudding of his heart.

Duncan groaned, a long sigh of thwarted desire. "Why do you torture me like this, Jayne? Is it your idea of fun?"

"I don't mean to torture you, Duncan," she murmured into his shoulder.

His fingers roamed across her back, leaving a scorching trail of fire, then slid down to clasp the molded softness of the warm flesh below.

"Then for pity's sake why do you refuse me?" he demanded huskily. "You want me every bit as much as I want you. Admit it!"

"Yes," she said helplessly. "I do."

Duncan gasped. "Then you'll let me make love to you? Oh, my beautiful Jayne, it will be so wonderful."

"No, I didn't mean that," she cried. "It would be wrong, terribly wrong."

"Wrong?" he echoed incredulously. "You . . . *you* can say that?"

Jayne froze, then slowly she raised her eyes to look at him. His lean features were gaunt and tense in the muted light of the silk-shaded bedside lamp. "You might as well go on and say exactly what you mean," she choked. "How can a woman *like me* say that? I'm the lowest of the low in your eyes, aren't I? Altogether beneath contempt."

"No," he denied. "That's not true."

"Then what *is* true?" she demanded. "Isn't that what you came to my room for tonight, Duncan, to tell me what you know about me? So you'd better get on with it."

He nodded and half turned away from her, pressing his hand to the back of his neck. "When my brother left this island three years ago it was in a rebellious spirit of rejection. I didn't blame him for being attracted to the idea of life in London—the bright lights and fast pace of things, the feeling of being where the action is. It was a phase I went through myself around the time I was at university. Only with Iain it was much stronger, more like an obsession. I knew that it was useless to try and talk him out of it. But I believed that in his heart he was a true Stewart of Kilraven, and that he would never abandon this island for good."

"Which he wouldn't have done, had he not met me? Is that what you're saying?"

Duncan made a helpless gesture of assent. "I just couldn't begin to understand when Iain broke the news about you . . . *after* your marriage had taken place. It seemed to me that my brother had completely lost his reason."

"Why, for goodness' sake?" asked Jayne. "Just because I was an actress?"

He shook his head. "Of course not! But there were any number of hints that it was a disastrous marriage. The fact that Iain refused to bring you home to Kilraven, even for a brief visit. He finally admitted to me on the phone that you flatly declined to come to this 'back of beyond,' as you described it. Furthermore, you'd made it very clear that I wouldn't be welcomed in London. I soon came to realize that the two of you were living at a ruinously expensive pace—because *you*, Jayne, insisted on renting a luxury apartment in Chelsea and throwing lavish parties."

With no memory to call upon, it was impossible for Jayne to deny any of this, and she could only say wretchedly, "But I must have loved Iain. I would never have married a man I didn't love."

"Love!" scoffed Duncan. "Perhaps the word has a different connotation in your sort of society. It certainly didn't mean that you were faithful to your husband. Apparently you had what it's fashionable to describe as an 'open' marriage."

"Oh no!" she moaned despairingly. "Are you really positive about that?"

"If you knew the circumstances of Iain's death," he said heavily, "you wouldn't need to ask."

"I do know the circumstances," she admitted, after a slight hesitation. "Sandy McFadden told me." But had Sandy edited his version of the story, she wondered, in order to spare her feelings as much as possible?

Duncan's look was charged with resentment. "You didn't even bother to inform me that my brother was dead. It was almost a fortnight before I heard the news from a friend, so I wasn't even permitted to attend his funeral. And you never answered any of my letters asking for details of his death. It was only when you discovered that Iain had left a string of debts—debts incurred mainly by *your* wild spending—that you decided to get in touch with me. From out of the blue I received notification that you were on your way to visit me—by cable! Which presumably was intended to give me no chance of preventing you from coming."

Devastated by these revelations about herself, Jayne kept silent for long seconds. When at last she spoke, it was with a tiny thread of a voice. "Would you have sent me away, Duncan, had it not been for the plane crash?"

He made a shrug with his hands. "How do I know? I fully intended to; I thought it no more than you deserved. But you were my brother's widow. Even though I owed *you* nothing, I had to consider what Iain would have wished. He must have loved you, after a fashion."

"You believe that, then?" Jayne was surprised, even a little gladdened.

Duncan met her gaze steadily. "From the first moment I saw you, lying in bed at the hospital, I understood what it was all about. The poor young devil must have been completely bewitched by you. He must have been driven insane by your beautiful face and desirable body. If I hadn't known the bitter truth about you, I myself would have felt the same. Once I'd set eyes on you, I couldn't find it in my heart to blame Iain anymore. I too wanted to possess you, quite desperately, and poor Iain didn't have the sort of willpower that I have, to help him avoid such a fatal trap."

"I didn't mean to trap you," Jayne protested miserably.

"No? Why else, then, did you come here? What exactly had you in mind when you set out on that fateful plane journey? Money, or marriage? Whichever it was, I haven't any doubt that it was to be extracted from me under your seductive spell. It had worked with one brother, you must have reasoned, so why not the other?"

"No, you're wrong!" Jayne was shaking her head violently from side to side. "I could never have been as calculating as that."

"How can you possibly know," he demanded cruelly, "when you remember nothing about the past?"

"I just *do* know," she insisted. Then, desperately floundering for words, she began, "Whatever may have been my intention, and, as you say, I can't be sure *what* I had in mind, I *am* certain of this. *After* the accident, after I recovered consciousness and you came to see me, well . . . none of those horrible things you've been saying about me have been true from that moment on. I give you my solemn word, Duncan, I'm not trying to trap you into *anything*." Looking into his eyes now was like gazing into the fiery heart of a furnace. But Jayne wouldn't flinch as she silently begged him to believe what she had said.

Duncan said slowly, thickly, "Then you are ready to give yourself to me, freely and willingly?"

"No . . . no, I didn't mean that."

He caught his breath impatiently. "You want me, Jayne, you've even admitted it to me—as if your body hadn't already betrayed the fact plainly. You've just insisted that you're *not* trying to extract a price for your favors. So what, in the name of heaven, is preventing us from making love?"

The fact, Jayne's heart screamed in protest, that I could never allow the man I love to possess my body when all he feels for me is desire. If only Duncan felt the tiniest spark of fondness for her—even tenderness would be enough—she would accept his lovemaking joyfully. There would be no strength in her to resist him. But the only emotions he felt apart from blatant desire were scorn and contempt.

She said woodenly, "I don't have to give you a reason."

Duncan's eyes sparked with anger, and Jayne felt afraid. And yet . . . not afraid. Something deep inside her was exulting, thrilling at his nearness, responding to the heady intoxication of the man. Her love for him was a flame that would not be quenched.

"Even now," he rasped thickly, "you still play the eternal feminine game. While your words deny me what I crave, your delectable body is being put to its most provocative use. You know exactly and precisely what a seductive picture you present in that satin robe, with only a diaphanous nightdress underneath.

"This is the middle of the night," she protested. "You virtually force your way into my room and then dare to accuse me of being provocative because I'm wearing nothing but a nightgown and a satin robe!"

Duncan moved quickly, as if some invisible shackle had snapped and set him free. Though Jayne tried to evade him, she was too late. With a groan he flung himself at her and crushed her in his arms. As his lips roved her face, from the smooth brow to the soft skin of her cheeks and ears, then down to her slender throat and the sculpted hollows of her neck, she felt the achingly familiar sense of longing suffuse her body. She was fighting a desperate battle with herself. Her treacherous body was screaming for fulfillment, for the ultimate ecstasy of loving, yet somehow by strength of will she must conquer her weakness and remain unyielding and unresponsive to Duncan's increasingly passionate caresses.

With impatient fingers he threw her robe open and pulled the thin satin ribbon of her nightgown strap, exposing her bare shoulder. His lips made a scorching trail on her naked flesh, and he buried his face in the secret valley between her breasts until Jayne wanted to cry out with the exquisite delight of it. Her fingers itched to tangle into his dark hair and cradle his head lovingly against the warm curves of her bosom. Somehow she managed to stifle the moans of pleasure that welled up from the depths of her being.

"You little she-devil!" Duncan breathed hoarsely. "By heaven, I'll make you drop this marble statue act and become the hot-blooded, vibrant woman you really are."

With a muttered oath he wrenched the shimmering robe away from her completely and let it crumple to a heap on the carpet. Jayne tried to gather the flimsy nightdress closer about her but to no avail. She heard the fabric rip as he tore it roughly from her body. When he swept her into his arms and carried her naked to the bed, she made no attempt to struggle. She could not hope to free herself from his superior strength, and she was terrified that to resist would only arouse him all the more.

Duncan threw her down onto the quilt and began to caress her bare flesh with savage roughness, as if he despised himself for wanting her. And all the while he exhorted her to respond. "For pity's sake, Jayne, for once in your life stop acting and be totally honest. You want me, we both know it, so why keep up this idiotic pretense?" He kissed her with a passionate violence that robbed her of breath, yet when at last he tore his lips away, she felt bereft. "Curse you, Jayne." He ground out the words. "Name your price, then! What do you want of me?"

Love! If only she could utter that one little word. She wanted Duncan's love, but that was a price he would never be willing to pay.

"I . . . I have no price," she whispered, and added the lie, "I want nothing from you, Duncan."

He pulled her harder to him till their bodies were welded together, their limbs entangled and entwined. Jayne lay rigid, knowing that by a single voluntary movement she would be lost, all chance of holding out against him swept away by the intensity of her desire.

"I could take you, if I wanted," he said through clenched teeth. "You know that, don't you?"

"Yes," she said tightly.

And if he did, what then? Would she, *could* she, remain the marble statue he had called her? Would not the act of sex with Duncan, however brutally indifferent he might be to her feelings, become for her an act of love?

Forcing out the words through the constriction of her throat, Jayne said, "If you don't let me go at once, Duncan, this very instant, I shall scream."

He tensed, becoming utterly still. "I believe you mean that."

"I most certainly do. And don't forget, you have guests staying in your house tonight. Do you want them to hear me?"

For a long moment Duncan remained motionless, his weight still crushing her into the softness of the bed. Then, with a smothered curse, he rolled off her and sat up. As if the sight of her nakedness offended him now, he pulled across the swansdown quilt until it covered her.

"I could have prevented you from screaming," he said huskily. "Didn't that occur to you?"

"Yes." Just the single bleak admission.

"And?"

"I . . . I thought that even you wouldn't . . ."

"Behave so badly?" he suggested. He gave a short, dry laugh. "Look to your own behavior, Jayne, before you use such a term about me. You employ every ounce of feminine allure you possess to smash down my defenses. You advance and retreat with the skill of a sorceress, knowing precisely the explosive effect you have on a man. You tempt him with your lovely body, offering the highest peaks of sensual ecstasy, and then hold back—until the poor fool is ready to capitulate. I know that I must be insane, completely out of my mind, but I give up and admit defeat. You want marriage, I suppose? Well, so be it."

In the muted light of the lamp, Jayne stared at him blankly. His face was drawn and haggard as he returned her gaze. "You . . . you mean you're prepared to marry me?" she gasped.

"Yes," he snapped.

"Without love?" she cried, outraged. "You're offering me marriage merely as a way of gratifying your sexual appetite?"

The tone of his bitter laugh made her shudder, there was such unfettered savagery in it. "I've never had the least difficulty in gratifying my sexual needs," he grated. "But what I feel now is something quite out of the ordinary, not the normal desire of a virile man. I am in the grip of a thirst that I shall never be able to slake, no matter how often I return to drink. Yes marriage, Jayne . . . that's the only possible answer for us both. It would provide you with what you want, and me with what I must have."

"No, no!" she spat at him. "It's a contemptible suggestion."

"Great heaven, do you still want more?" he groaned. "What, then? Surely not for me to leave Kilraven and live with you in London? I could never abandon my island and its people, no matter what it cost me."

"I'm not asking you to leave Kilraven," she said despairingly. "Can't you understand, Duncan? I'm asking *nothing* of you, and I have nothing to offer."

Except love, an inner voice protested. Even now, even after his monstrous proposal, she still had a heart full of love that she longed to lay at his feet.

Duncan stood up, his lean jaw thrust forward with anger. His voice was like the crack of a leather whip. "What pleasure it must have given you, to reduce me to bargaining for your body. But you've just gone too far, Jayne . . . you've overstepped the limit and it's brought me to my senses. I wouldn't marry you now for anything in the world. How I wish to heaven that I had never set eyes on you!"

Goaded beyond endurance, Jayne sat up on the bed and drew the quilt about her. She gave Duncan a hard, challenging look. "What you really mean is that you wish I had died in that plane crash, along with the others."

There was a long, long pause. Then at last Duncan broke the waiting silence. "Yes," he said quietly, "I think I do! It would have been better for us both."

Chapter Nine

She had to be practical, she had to be!

Jayne awoke early the next morning with this thought drumming in her mind. What was she to do now? It was impossible to envisage returning to London and trying to pick up the threads of her former life—an ultra-sophisticated style of life that now filled her with disgust. In any case, she remembered, not only had she no money to her name, but countless debts awaited her in London.

Possibly, by now, Duncan would be so anxious to see her gone that he would no longer raise any objection to her taking the job at the hospital. But even if that were the case, would she be able to endure living in such close proximity to the man she loved? On a clear day she would be able to look across the water and see Kilraven, knowing that Duncan was there—so near and yet so infinitely beyond her reach. And, no doubt, from time to time, she would actually meet him face to face in the little town of Craigmond.

Yet how could she go anywhere else, without friends or money? She had been an actress, she reminded herself. Was that a career to which she could return? Had she any contacts from the past that could be put to good use now?

The thought was unappealing in the extreme. She would be reduced to begging favors on the strength of a previous association from people she couldn't even remember. And what hope was there, anyway? Unemployment in the acting profession was notoriously high, and she had no confidence that she could make a favorable impression on producers and casting directors. The mere thought of appearing before the public on a stage was terrifying to her now.

Of one thing she was quite positive, she would ask no favors from Duncan. That would be too humiliating. Racking her brain, she could think of only one other person in the world to whom she could turn. Sandy McFadden. It seemed unfair to take advantage of his obvious fondness for her when she knew she had nothing beyond friendship to offer him in return. But needs must! She would explain very carefully to Sandy that whatever he did to help her would be repaid just as soon as she found her feet. He might perhaps lend her sufficient money to keep her going for a week or two, until she found a job somewhere far away from the Isle of Kilraven.

Jayne remained in her room until she knew that breakfast would be finished. She had no appetite, nor could she face the prospect of meeting the others at table. It was past nine-thirty, therefore, when she descended the staircase and crossed to the telephone lobby in the Great Hall.

Before she reached it, though, Duncan appeared

through a doorway. Jayne cursed her bad luck in running into him at this juncture. Unlike herself, he looked clear-eyed and alert, unaffected by the events of the previous night. "Good morning, Jayne," he greeted her. "We didn't see you at breakfast. And neither, I gather from Callum Blair, did you ring for a tray in your room."

"I didn't want any breakfast," she explained in despair, because just talking to Duncan like this was making her heart thud alarmingly.

"You mustn't start missing meals," he reproved her. "Considering that you're still a convalescent, it's important for you to take care of yourself." He fixed her with a glance. "Who are you intending to phone?"

Unable to think of any way of avoiding a direct answer, she mumbled, "Sandy McFadden, as a matter of fact."

Duncan raised his eyebrows questioningly. "Is your health bothering you? Do you want professional medical advice?"

"No, nothing like that. I . . . I just want to talk to him."

"Indeed? Are you feeling lonely, Jayne? I'd have thought there was sufficient company for you here just now, with the McEwans staying."

"If you must know," she said, in as brisk a voice as she could summon, "I want to ask Sandy about ways and means for me to leave Kilraven."

"But there's no need to trouble Dr. McFadden. Nothing could be easier to arrange. When did you have in mind going?"

Astonished that Duncan seemed to be so amenable, Jayne said, "This morning; the sooner the better."

He considered for a moment. "Dougal can take you across the Sound, and wait to bring you back. I imagine that your errand won't take long?"

"But . . . but I'm not coming back," she stammered.

Duncan's face hardened to granite. "Of course you are!"

"But what's the point?" she asked, with an unhappy sigh. "After . . . after last night, the only possible thing is for me to go right away."

Unaccountably—and to her utter dismay—Duncan shook his head decidedly. "For the time being, your place is here."

"Why?" she flared. "Just because you have some peculiar notion of keeping up appearances as a man who does the right thing by his widowed sister-in-law? The time for that is long since past."

"It's not a matter of keeping up appearances for my sake, Jayne. But how can you think of being so downright discourteous to Robbie and Agnes Mac-Leod?"

She looked at him in bewilderment. "How could I be discourteous to the MacLeods by going away? What can it matter to them what I do?"

"Have you forgotten?" he demanded. "Tonight is the *ceilidh* to celebrate their silver wedding." He pronounced the Gaelic word for party as *kayley*. "Everyone on the island will be coming, and if the laird or any of his houseguests were to stay away, it would be regarded as a deliberate insult."

"But surely you could explain?"

"Explain what? Just how do you propose that I should put the matter to them—and everyone else?"

"You could always tell the truth," she said almost choking.

"And what exactly, to your mind, *is* the truth?" he inquired.

"That your outrageous behavior left me no alternative but to leave your house," she said, the huskiness of her voice betraying her nervousness.

"And am I to include your own part in it?"

"My . . . my part?" She faltered.

"That you acted like a wanton, bewitching me into such a state that I was ready to promise you anything. Can you deny it, Jayne?"

Her eyes fell before the implacable challenge of his gaze. To her surprise, though, his voice was gentler when he spoke again. Gentler, but ringing with unarguable authority.

"You will stay for the *ceilidh* tonight, and for the small dinner party the MacLeods are giving tomorrow night for me and my guests. After that . . . well, we shall see."

"But you can't expect me to—"

"I do expect it, Jayne! So, for the present, you had better forget about calling Dr. McFadden. In fact, you had better drop any idea of calling him at all. What do you imagine he could do to help you?"

"He . . . he's a friend."

"Is that how you imagine he sees himself?" he inquired ironically.

"I don't know," she countered.

"Then you're highly unobservant, Jayne. When I broke in on you two the other day, a single glance was enough to tell me precisely what McFadden is hoping for. Are you planning to play upon the poor man's susceptibilities? Have you no conscience at all? A woman like you could wreck the whole life of a decent, straightforward chap like Sandy McFadden."

Jayne flushed scarlet at the implication of his words. Through her anger, she said shakily, "I'd make it perfectly clear to Sandy that I was asking his help as a friend—and nothing more!"

"And that, you suggest, would prevent him from hoping for a great deal more? Stop fooling yourself, Jayne."

Before she had a chance to reply the phone rang, and Duncan picked it up. He talked for a few moments about some business matter, then asked the caller to hold. Turning back to Jayne, he said, "Now go to the small dining room, and I'll tell Callum to bring you coffee and toast. No, don't argue, just do as I say. You must start the day with some food inside you."

Jayne hesitated, wanting to refuse to obey his brusque instructions. But she felt too weak to argue with him anymore.

To fill in the remainder of the morning, she went for a long, solitary walk along the rocky eastern shore of the island. She was in a mutinous mood. And yet, behind this, she felt a curious sense of relief. The prospect before her had been bleak and uncertain. Now, for the next few days at least, she did not have to plan ahead. She would be remaining here on Kilraven. Incredibly, after all that had happened, the thought of this could still lighten her heart.

Over lunch, the conversation turned to the Mac-Leods' *ceilidh*. "It's to be held in the hay barn near their house," Duncan explained. "There'll be bales of barley straw to sit on, and trestle tables for the food and drink." He grinned at Fiona and her mother. "I suggest that you don't put on your daintiest dresses, but something a little more practical."

Fiona made a little moue of disgust. "It all sounds horribly primitive, I must say."

"It's not the ballroom of the Gleneagles Hotel," Duncan agreed. "But *ceilidhs* are always good fun. And what's more, it's a fine opportunity for everyone on the island to mix on terms of equality."

This thought seemed to have little appeal to Fiona. "I hope that doesn't mean you'll expect me to dance with crofters and their ilk?"

"Why shouldn't you?" He glanced at Jayne. "Do *you* have any objection?"

She could not help coloring as his penetrating gaze rested on her, and she attempted to cover up with an uncaring shrug. "I shan't know any of the dances, but I'll certainly do my best to join in."

Was it only her imagination, or did Duncan's expression soften just a little? She had no time to ponder the point, for Lady McEwan had turned to address Fiona and herself.

"I've promised Agnes MacLeod that I'll help with the preparations this afternoon by doing some floral decorations," she said. "Would you two girls care to join me?"

"Count me out!" snapped Fiona, the disgust on her face conveying the thought that she could find far better ways of spending her time.

Jayne noticed Fiona's mother's hurt look. Summoning up a pretended enthusiasm, she said brightly, "I'd like to come, Lady McEwan. Thank you for suggesting it."

And so the two of them set out in a land rover, that being the most suitable vehicle for the rocky track leading to the MacLeods' house two miles away. Lady McEwan, despite her elegant appearance, handled the vehicle expertly, almost as if born to the life. "This sort of country really does one's heart good," she remarked fervently, as they drove across a stretch of moorland alongside a cascading stream that glinted in the sunlight.

"Yes," Jayne replied, a painful lump in her throat.

The older woman spared a moment to glance at her. "You love it here, don't you, my dear?"

"Yes, I do," she admitted.

"I never thought that I would myself," Lady McEwan continued. "When Douglas suggested retiring to this remote area I was appalled. Yet when we actually came, I felt at home from the very beginning. I imagine it's been much the same for you, Jayne, although of course you can't remember your life in London."

"It's true that I could be happy living in a place like this," she said sadly, fiddling nervously with the gold band of her wedding ring. "But I shan't be staying, Lady McEwan. A few more days, at the very most, and then I'll be away."

"Duncan will miss you," the older woman said in an even tone.

"Oh no, I don't think so," Jayne responded. "I'm no more than an irritating problem to Duncan. He'll be thankful to see me gone."

Lady McEwan tutted in protest. "I'm quite sure that you're wrong about that, my dear. After all, you are his brother's widow, and family feeling runs strong with the Stewarts of Kilraven. He's a fine man, is Duncan."

"Yes," Jayne agreed tonelessly.

Fortunately, they were nearing the end of their short journey. Ahead, the track snaked down toward a small, sturdily built house with cleanly whitewashed walls that positively sparkled in the crystal-clear light. Nearby stood the large thatched barn where the *ceilidh* was to take place. When Lady McEwan cut the engine, Jayne could hear a cheerful babble of voices coming from inside.

Entering, they found Agnes directing several other women, among them one or two crofters' wives whom Jayne recognized. Some were sweeping the earthen floor, and others were setting up long trestle tables for the food and drink. A space in the center was left clear for dancing.

Now that she was here Jayne found she was glad to have something to take her mind off her problems.

While Lady McEwan and Agnes made elaborate arrangements of spring flowers, she brought in great armfuls of the greenery, which a tractor had piled outside the door, and began festooning it around the barn—large sprays of larch and flowering rowan, and some newly unfurling beech leaves.

She was standing high on a stepladder, winding trails of ivy around a heavy roof beam, when suddenly, from out of the shadows above her, a pair of green eyes glinted. The fleeting moment of shock passed, and Jayne realized with amusement that it was a cat.

"Here, puss!" she called, and clucked her tongue invitingly.

The cat, innately suspicious, remained motionless. But when she repeated the invitation in a caressing voice, it leaped down lithely from its high perch and landed on the beam beside her with a soft thud of paws. It was a lovely orange tabby, its coat gleaming with cleanliness. Jayne tickled the thick fur behind its ear, and the cat purred ecstatically, performing a curious little wriggle of delight.

"What a pretty puss you are, Samantha," she said, then stopped abruptly. Why had she used that name? But it seemed right, somehow. Then, almost like a shutter clicking in her brain, she was no longer in the dim recesses of the barn but outside in the open air shielding the sunlight from her eyes as she reached up for the orange tabby on the branch of an old apple tree.

Heart pounding, Jayne scarcely dared to breathe. She clung desperately to the tantalizing vision as she fondled the cat. An apple tree in full blossom . . . a white garden fence nearby, and below it a bed of wallflowers—she could actually smell their fragrance drifting on the warm air.

Then the shutters of her mind snapped shut again

and the vivid scene was snatched away from her. Perched as she was on the stepladder, the sudden transition to blankness left Jayne giddy. She swayed and gave a little gasp of dismay as she felt herself falling. . . .

Strong arms caught her and set her gently on her feet.

"There, there, poor wee lassie! Did ye come over a bit faint?" It was Robbie MacLeod, who had been fixing a string of colored lights right beside her. In relief she clung to his broad frame as her swirling senses righted themselves.

"A very neat performance, Jayne," drawled a voice behind her. "I've really got to hand it to you!"

She spun around, releasing herself from the factor's arms. "Fiona! I . . . I thought you weren't coming this afternoon."

"Are you disappointed?" The lovely green eyes were gleaming with mockery.

"Fiona came with *me*," said another voice, and Jayne looked past Fiona's shoulder to see Duncan standing there. "I had to deliver some crates of beer and she decided to come along too." He took a step foward and studied Jayne's face. "What made you suddenly feel dizzy?"

"Just for a few moments I thought . . ." But she trailed off uncertainly. What use was it to tell them that for a few heart-stopping moments she had thought that her memory might be coming back? "It was nothing," she finished with a little shrug.

"You're okay now?" persisted Duncan.

"Yes, I'm fine!" She turned to the factor. "Thanks a lot for catching me, Mr. MacLeod."

"That's all right, lassie. It was lucky I was on the spot."

"Yes, wasn't it?" Fiona slipped in dryly. "You

couldn't have timed that fall better, Jayne, if you'd rehearsed it for hours."

A hot protest rose to Jayne's lips, but somehow she managed to stifle it. "Well, if you'll forgive me I'll get on with hanging up this greenery," she said.

"Not on the stepladder, you won't," Duncan retorted grimly. "You mustn't risk another fall. I'll climb up, and you can hand me up the sprays and tell me how you want them fixed."

Fiona looked furious. "For heaven's sake, Duncan," she protested, "you're supposed to be unloading those crates we brought over. I want to get out of this place, it's so gloomy and creepy."

"Then ask someone else to do the crates," he replied offhandedly. "I won't be very long."

With an impatient exclamation Fiona swung on her heel and stalked out. It was obvious that she had no intention of soiling her hands with anything that could be called work.

Duncan mounted the stepladder and absently tickled the cat, which was still perched on the beam. "Now, Jayne, how do you want this arranged?" he asked pleasantly.

It was unfair, unnerving. Her chief reason for coming this afternoon had been to get well out of Duncan's way for a few hours. And now he was here, too, working right beside her. As he reached down for another spray of ivy their fingers touched, and the fleeting contact sent sharp tingles of excitement racing through her veins.

Robbie MacLeod had strung his colored lights across to the far end of the barn and was fixing a loop there. None of the women helpers were within hearing. Duncan paused in what he was doing and looked down at her, the planes and angles of his face half lost in shadow. "Jayne, about last night . . ."

She went very still, feeling a tight knot of pain around her heart. For long seconds the silence hung between them. Then he went on huskily, "Ever since . . . I've been through hell."

"Don't you think that I have, too?" The words trailed out of her, with only sadness, not bitterness.

"Yes, I suppose so." Duncan remained unmoving, poised four steps above her. "I just wanted to say . . ."

From the open doorway of the barn, Fiona called irritably, "Duncan, haven't you finished yet? For goodness sake, get a move on."

"Coming!" he called, his dark gaze still resting on Jayne. Then, with a shrug, he muttered, "I suppose that we've already said everything there is to be said between us."

Checking that the greenery he'd fixed was quite secure, he climbed down. With just a curt nod at Jayne, he strode away and disappeared through the doorway.

Yes, everything had already been said. *I wouldn't marry you now if you went down on your hands and knees and begged me to. I wish to heaven that I'd never set eyes on you at all.* He would rather she had died in that plane crash. He'd actually admitted it!

Callum and Isobel Blair were to attend the *ceilidh*, and Jayne volunteered to go with them in the land rover to ease the crush in the car.

"But they'll be leaving early for Isobel to take her contribution to the refreshments," Duncan protested. "There's plenty of room in my car for five."

"Oh, let the girl do what she wants," said Fiona impatiently, and he didn't pursue the point.

The party was already in full swing when Jayne arrived with the Blairs. After offering Robbie and Agnes MacLeod her congratulations on their twenty-five years of marriage, she lost herself among the gathering crowd. The barn, with its colored lights and decorations looked most festive, and the trestle tables all but groaned with food . . . platters of cold meats, sandwiches, oatcakes and hot potatoes baked in their jackets. There were sweet things too—trifles and Scotch pancakes and delicious-looking buttery short-breads. And on a silver stand an enormous iced cake. To drink, there was ale and whiskey galore, with fruit cordials for those who preferred them, and tea and coffee also.

A fiddle and an accordion struck up a lively tune, and at once a young man approached Jayne and boldly asked her to dance. He was darkly handsome, with gleaming black hair and a devil-may-care glint in his eyes.

"I'm afraid that I don't know the proper steps," she said with a smile, "but I'm willing to have a go."

"Oh, you'll manage fine," he said, taking her hand and leading her to the cleared space in the center. "I'm Neil Guthrie, by the way, and of course I know who you are."

Neil informed her that he owned his own fishing boat—a fact of which he was clearly very proud—but apart from this there was little chance for them to talk during the energetic reel. However, he conveyed his admiration by the way he let his peat-brown eyes linger on her face and figure.

When the dance ended everyone clapped loudly. Neil draped his arm companionably around Jayne's shoulders and led her off to find refreshment. As they were pushing their way through the crush she noticed that the party from Kilraven House had finally arrived. Duncan seemed to pick her out at once in the bright yellow dress she was wearing, and she felt his eyes piercing her with scorn. Does he think I'm a wanton, she cried in inward protest, just because I agreed to dance with a handsome young mman? Who was it, after all, who had virtually forced her to attend the *ceilidh* tonight? And furthermore, he had made it clear that he *expected* her to dance with the islanders. All the same, under the compelling force of those ebony-black eyes, she slipped from Neil's clasp.

Excusing herself with a smile, she left the youth and went to join a group of women, crofters' wives she had come to know. Since the episode of Lady's injury, Jayne felt quite at ease with them. But all the while she chatted, she was disturbingly aware of Duncan's presence. Wherever he happened to be in the barn, his striking kilted figure seemed to be directly in her view. Though Fiona tried to monopolize him, Jayne noticed that he spread himself around, having a word with everyone, dancing with a different partner each time. At one point silence was called for while Duncan made a presentation to the happy hosts of a fine antique grandfather clock, a silver wedding gift to which all the islanders had contributed. Robbie MacLeod, amid much teasing and laughter, made a rather shy thank-you speech and then, to a roar of approval, turned and gave his wife a hearty kiss.

A cry went up from one corner and was promptly echoed on all sides. "Kilraven must gi'e us a song!"

At first demurring, Duncan smilingly gave way and stepped forward into a space which had been cleared for him. Utter silence fell as he began to sing in a fine rich baritone voice, unaccompanied by any instrument. He looked magnificent, Jayne thought with a catch in her throat, in his kilt of Stewart tartan, with a jabot of lace at his neck and silver buckles on his shoes.

The song was in Gaelic, so Jayne couldn't understand a single word. But that didn't matter. She knew instinctively that it was a story of wistful longing, a song of the sweet, aching sadness of love. She listened enthralled till the beautifully pure flow of sound came to an end, the final notes dying into a hushed silence. Then a storm of applause broke out, with a stomping of feet and cries of "Bravo!"

When the music struck up again, Jayne saw Duncan making his way across to her, an obvious duty, she knew, performed for the benefit of onlookers. As his hand lightly touched her shoulder, she gave an involuntary shiver and drew back a little. She saw Duncan's jaw tighten, but he made no comment.

Without any intention of complimenting him, she found herself saying, "That was a really lovely song, Duncan, and you sang it magnificently."

He tilted his head. "Thank you, Jayne."

"It was very sad; a lament, I suppose you'd call it."

His eyebrows shot up. "Is this another of your sudden discoveries . . . that you understand Gaelic?"

"No, not a word. But I could somehow feel the meaning coming through to me." She hesitated, then ventured, "It's to do with the parting of two lovers, I suppose?"

Duncan's eyes flickered. "The singer is swearing that come what may—even if they are fated never to meet again as long as they live—he pledges his eternal devotion. His eternal fidelity. Do you find the thought too cloyingly romantic when translated into English?"

Jayne met his gaze, but had to glance away. "I find it very touching," she murmured.

The dance this time was not one of the Scottish steps, but a waltz, a slow, dreamy tune, and she and Duncan moved in perfect unison. Jayne tried to tell herself that the man who held her in his arms was no more important to her than the young fisherman Neil Guthrie had been. To no avail! Her skin, her whole being, thrilled to his touch and she was filled with elation. She wished that she could spin out these enchanted moments to fill the rest of her life. It wasn't real—she knew that—but while they moved in unison, their bodies touching, she could make believe that it was real, make believe that Duncan loved her as she loved him.

"Jayne," he said softly, "you and I have got to talk."

"Talk?"

"We can't leave things between us as they were last night," he said. "It would be intolerable for you to leave Kilraven with such bad blood between us. Perhaps, after all, you need not go."

The warm illusion of harmony was shattered and harsh reality came rushing back. "How can I possibly stay?" she said despairingly.

Into her line of vision swam a pair of feline green eyes. Fiona, partnered by Robbie MacLeod, was watching them jealously. She would be utterly ruthless in her determination to keep the Laird of Kilraven for herself. Suppose, Jayne thought tormentedly, that last night she had accepted Duncan's rash proposal of marriage, torn from him though it was in a frenzied bid to possess her body? Would he have honored it in the cold light of morning, when he had got what he wanted? Or would he have cast her aside like an old shoe in favor of Fiona McEwan?

Jayne shivered in Duncan's arms, and he asked quickly, "Are you cold?"

"No. . . ." She stopped dancing, saying, "Please . . . I'd prefer to sit this out."

"Right. Let's go over to that corner where it's less crowded."

"No, don't come with me," Jayne protested. "You're expected to mingle, not to spend time with your sister-in-law."

Duncan hesitated a moment, then nodded. "We'll

talk tomorrow morning," he said firmly. "We'll get everything sorted out."

With the cheerful noise of the party in her ears, Jayne sat alone in her secluded corner, thankful to be half-concealed by a big array of leaves and ferns. Coming to the *ceilidh* tonight had been an intolerable ordeal, and it was a relief to relax and let her mind drift. . . .

She found herself staring fixedly at a square red tin box, tucked out of sight behind a straw bale, in which someone had brought their contribution of food. Printed in bold white lettering was the name of the product it had originally contained, Crowther's Crackers. The two words nudged oddly at Jayne's mind, stirring some latent memory that she could not grasp.

Crowther . . . why did that name disturb her so? She felt invaded by a curious fluttering excitement, as if she were on the brink of something momentous.

At the far end of the barn someone started to play the bagpipes. As the preliminary drone began, it seemed to reach Jayne's ears as the droning of an engine. Suddenly she was no longer in the hay barn, but in the cabin of a small aircraft. There was someone in the seat beside her, a girl, and they were both looking down at the fascinating scene below, a sparkling, deep blue ocean, dotted with foam-fringed islands.

With a muttered curse a heavy body jolted against her, and something wet splashed her dress. Jayne felt herself falling, falling, hurtling precipitously through a dark, terrifying spiral, while panic screamed in her mind. Then darkness, followed by an explosion of dazzling white light. Of understanding!

Neil Guthrie was apologizing to her profusely. "Ach, I'm that sorry, Mrs. Stewart, I am indeed! I spotted you sitting alone in this corner, and I thought you might care for a drink. But like a clumsy fool I tripped over my own feet. Just look at your lovely dress, all wet and stained!" He pulled out a large white handkerchief and began dabbing at her skirt rather ineffectively. "I just canna tell you how sorry I am, Mrs. Stewart."

"It doesn't matter," she murmured, scarcely hearing him. Her brain, so empty of memories until this moment, was suddenly so brimful of them that she felt hopelessly bewildered. One thing she clung to, gasping out in wondrous excitement, "My name is Crowther . . . Nerissa Crowther!"

Neil scratched his head in confusion. "Eh, what's that, Mrs. Stewart? Is it what you were called before you wed Mr. Iain?"

"No, not that. It's my name *now*. Oh, what a relief!"

She wanted to stand up and shout out loud for everyone to hear that at last she had found herself. But it was still too new and fragile, this knowledge that she was not Jayne Stewart at all. She needed time, time on her own, to piece everything together and make a complete person of herself.

She stood up, and the floor seemed to dip and sway beneath her. "I . . . I'm going outside. I need some fresh air."

"I'll come with you," said Neil.

"No! Please . . . I just want to be alone for a little while."

Fortunately there was a small side door through which she could slip out unnoticed. Neil let her go reluctantly, and she could feel his puzzled gaze on her back.

She had expected it to be dark outside, for there was no moon tonight. But instead a curious, luminous glow hung over the silent landscape. It was as if the sky were draped with long curtains of colored light that flickered mysteriously—from the cold blue of ice to the crimson-orange of leaping flame, with cross beams of glacial green flashing slantwise.

The *Aurora Borealis*, of course, the Northern Lights. She felt a little scared before this majestic display of natural forces. And yet she felt uplifted too. It seemed almost as if the very heavens themselves were marking as an event of great significance her metamorphosis from Jayne Stewart to Nerissa Crowther.

Chapter Ten

"Jayne, where are you, Jayne?"

Duncan's voice, borne toward her with a drift of fragrant breeze, made the girl sitting on an old drystone wall go rigidly tense.

The past was quite clear in her mind now, dazzlingly clear. She was not Jayne Stewart at all, and the knowledge should have made her jubilant. But it didn't. She, Nerissa Crowther, was here on Kilraven under false pretenses. Duncan Stewart had taken her beneath his wing purely from a sense of family obligation, when in reality she had no claim on him whatsoever.

He was moving away from her now, his resonant voice growing fainter. She felt torn in two, wishing desperately that she had never met the Laird of Kilraven. She was terrified of facing Duncan again, lest she break down and burst into tears at the prospect of leaving this idyllic island and never seeing him again.

Loving him so desperately was a burden she would have to carry for the rest of her life.

How could she get away, escape the island without a painful encounter with Duncan? Dare she sneak back into the barn to find Neil Guthrie, and beg him to take her to the mainland in his fishing boat? But how could she explain her urgent need to go now, at once? Besides, as an islander Neil was dependent upon the laird's goodwill. Would he be willing to do anything that might incur Duncan's wrath?

And once in Craigmond, what was she to do then, with no money for a hotel room? It just wouldn't be fair to involve Sandy McFadden. There was the vet on the Isle of Lewis, of course; she could phone him. But what would he think of a midnight call from a girl who had been reported dead in the plane crash?

With each passing second a fresh problem darted into her mind. Arms hugged around herself, she stared unhappily across the dark glistening waters of the Sound. Her memory was fully returned now, and the truth about herself was far better than she could possibly have imagined, releasing her in one fell swoop from the shame of being Jayne Stewart. Her real past was one that she could happily accept and live with—yet the future was bleak indeed.

"Jayne!" Duncan's voice from right behind her brought her leaping to her feet. "What on earth do you think you're doing," he demanded, "sitting out here in the chill night air? Come back inside at once."

As Duncan went to take her arm, she shrank back in alarm from the disturbingly sweet promise of his touch. "No, I . . . I can't."

"Can't?" In the weirdly flickering light his face was etched with deep concern. He said softly, "Are you all right, Jayne? I've just heard the craziest story from Neil Guthrie. He's a bit the worse for wear, of course, but he insists that you told him your name was something quite different."

"It's true," she confirmed, her breath coming jerkily. "The whole thing has been a terrible mistake. Jayne Stewart was killed in that accident. I . . . I was sitting next to her after we changed planes at Glasgow, and when it . . ." She closed her eyes, fighting to shut out the horrifyingly vivid memories of those last fateful moments. Ringing in her ears was the deafening explosion as the plane burst into flames behind her just as she had leaped down from the escape hatch and was scrambling away to safety through a patch of brambles. She felt guilty, somehow, at having been the only one to survive. "I . . . I'm afraid that Jayne didn't make it in time," she finished bleakly.

There was a long breathless silence. Then Duncan said in a tense voice, "But I don't understand . . . you had that photograph of Iain and myself in your pocket."

"She—Jayne—had been showing it to me; I remember that distinctly. I suppose that as the plane dived I must have thrust it into my jacket pocket without thinking."

Duncan passed a hand across his brow. "If you're not my sister-in-law, then who are you?"

"My name is Nerissa Crowther," she said, "and I'm a veterinary surgeon."

"You're a vet! So that explains how you knew exactly what to do about Lady's shoulder injury."

"Yes," she whispered.

"But what were you doing aboard a small shuttle plane to the Western Isles?" Duncan asked.

"I was traveling to take up a post on the Isle of Lewis. Up until now, I've been working in London, but I was never really happy there. You see, I was born and bred in Cornwall, but both my parents died while I was at veterinary college and after that I just couldn't face going back to live in the West Country. So I took the first job I was offered after I graduated last year, which happened to be in an animal welfare clinic in London. It was interesting work but I could never settle to city life, and when I spotted an advertisement for a qualified assistant on the Isle of Lewis, I applied at once and got the job. Only I never reached there. My new employer believes that I'm dead, of course."

She heard Duncan draw in a long, deep breath. "You haven't yet mentioned your husband."

"My husband?" she said, puzzled.

"You wear a wedding ring and an engagement ring," he pointed out.

"Oh, those!" Nerissa fingered the two rings lovingly, understanding why in the days when she had thought herself to be Jayne they had always brought her a sense of comfort. "They were my mother's," she explained to Duncan. "I wore them on the journey because that seemed the safest way to carry them. They're very precious to me, and I didn't want to take the risk of packing them and perhaps losing my luggage."

Duncan took a half step nearer to her. She couldn't see his eyes, but his voice had a breathless quality. "Does that mean that you're *not* married?"

"No," she answered softly, "I'm not married."

There had been a time, though, when she had seriously wondered whether to accept Richard Ebborn's oft-repeated proposal. He was in love with her, and he kept begging her to agree to marry him just as soon as his divorce went through. But she had known deep down in her heart that Richard wasn't the right man for her. She realized that, fond though she had become of him, her feelings fell short of the all-consuming love, which to her was essential for marriage. The final parting had come one afternoon when they were walking together on Hampstead Heath. On a bridge across a little stream, she had stopped and found the courage to tell Richard that it was best if they didn't see each other anymore . . . a significant moment in her life, which had returned to her in another tantalizing flash of memory. And in those other fragments of memory, her unseen companion had been Richard Ebborn, not Iain Stewart, as she had believed.

Duncan peeled off his evening jacket and wrapped it around her shoulders. As the lingering warmth of his body in the velvet fabric touched her bare arms, she gave a little shiver.

"Come on . . . Nerissa," he said softly, and it seemed almost as if he was savoring the name with pleasure.

"No, no. I can't return to the party!" she cried in sudden panic.

"I'm not asking you to. I couldn't myself, not now." He reached out and took her by the hand. "I'll put you in the car, then I'll go and tell Robbie that you're not feeling up to any more this evening; he'll understand. We'll go back to the house."

She was already seated in the car and Duncan had turned toward the barn when a thought struck her, and she called after him, "What about Sir Douglas and Lady McEwan—and Fiona? How will they get back?"

"I'll ask Robbie to bring them in his car later on. You and I need some time alone, to sort things out."

They drove back to Kilraven House in silence, each locked in their own thoughts. Sitting beside Duncan in the car, snuggled in the warmth of his jacket, she wished that this short journey could last forever. She wished that there was no need for explanations, no need for making plans, but that she could just continue like this, sitting beside the man she loved.

Duncan took her straight to the ladies' parlor, where

he stirred the logs in the stone hearth into a cheerful blaze. Then he poured her a small shot of brandy and told her to drink it down.

"It'll do you good," he said. "This has been a traumatic evening for you."

"Yes," she agreed, sipping. She was hanging on to each precious moment, holding herself cocooned in the warmth of Duncan's presence, not daring to look ahead to the bleak world that lay beyond.

"For me, too," he added.

She nodded slowly. "Yes, I suppose it must have been. To have taken me into your home and offered me protection, only to find that I'm a fraud. . . ."

"A fraud, Nerissa?"

"I mean, as your supposed sister-in-law, I had some sort of claim on your charity. But now . . ."

"Now," Duncan said huskily, "you have a claim on my heart." He came quickly and sat beside her on the sofa, taking her hands between his own. "You have done a wonderful thing this evening; you have made it possible for me to respect myself again. My sister-in-law Jayne Stewart is dead, so I should try not to speak ill of her. But the fact remains that she was a selfish and extravagant woman who was utterly ruthless in getting what she wanted. Yet even so, believing *you* to be that woman, I nevertheless found myself irresistibly drawn to you. I fought desperately against my desire for you, my longing to possess you—you can't imagine what a battle I fought with my better instincts. I tried to tell myself that what I felt for you was no more than a normal man's appetite for an attractive woman—which could surely be assuaged elsewhere. I had Fiona to turn to—right here in the house—and as you so rightly pointed out, she would have been only too willing and eager. Yet once I had met you, Fiona meant less than nothing to me. It was you I wanted, you I had to have if

I was not to go out of my mind with thwarted desire. At times I argued with myself that you were an utterly contemptible woman, that it would be no more than you deserved if I made use of your body for my pleasure. Yet always, Nerissa, it was for *myself* that I felt disgust, not you. Time and again the truth came stabbing through—the truth I couldn't bring myself to face."

"The . . . the truth?" She faltered.

"That I loved you. How was it possible that I had fallen in love with such a woman as Jayne Stewart? I kept asking myself. Just as my poor brother Iain had been blindly infatuated with the worthless Jayne, the same thing was happening to me. Every time you begged to be allowed to leave Kilraven, I decided it was nothing more than a devilish feminine ploy to ensnare me even more deeply. Nerissa, I must know . . . can you find it in your heart to forgive me, or have I made you hate me beyond redemption?"

"Hate you?" she echoed dazedly. "But I don't hate you, Duncan. How ever can you think such a thing?"

The grip of his hands tightened. "Then there's hope for me? Is it possible that you'll be able to forget the terrible, cruel things I've said to you and come to love me in return?"

Her senses swimming, Nerissa gazed into the dark pools of his eyes. "I love you *now,* Duncan. I have loved you, I think, ever since the moment I woke up and saw you in the hospital."

"But the names I called you, the way I behaved . . . !"

"It made me miserable," she admitted, "but it didn't stop me from loving you. Nothing could stop me loving you, Duncan."

For long moments, while time stood still, they looked at one another with incredulous understanding. Then, slowly, Duncan drew her into his arms and cradled her close, murmuring soft, caressing words of love. When his lips found hers, the kiss was sweet and tender, a promise of the passion to come.

Presently Duncan drew back and said shakily, "What a fool I was, not to have known that you couldn't be that kind of woman. . . ."

She pressed her fingertips to his lips. "How *could* you have known," she whispered, "when even I myself believed it?"

Duncan smiled his gratitude. "I love you, my darling. I love you beyond imagination. You cannot know the joy it is to hold you in my arms and admit it to you."

The radiance of the night sky that lay outside the drawn curtains seemed to have invaded the room. As they kissed again, she wound her arms around his neck and felt the sure, strong pulse of his heartbeat.

"It's time that Kilraven had a lady for its laird," he murmured against her silk-soft hair. "You will marry me, my darling?"

She smiled. "Of course I'll marry you."

Sweet minutes later, he said, "There will be various things to sort out in setting straight your identity. And we'll have to phone that vet on Lewis to tell him that he must find another assistant."

"He's probably set about doing that already," she said wryly. "But we must fetch my belongings, Duncan. I had a trunk sent on ahead of me, with clothes and things from my parents' home."

He took her hand and kissed each separate finger lovingly. "These are pretty rings you're wearing, my darling, but you'll forgive me if I insist on replacing them with rings that I'll buy for you. We'll have a few days in Edinburgh and get your trousseau at the same time. Where would you like to go for our honeymoon, darling? Italy, Greece, the United States? Wherever you say."

"Oh, Duncan." She laughed happily. "I just can't believe that this is really and truly happening."

"Oh, yes, it is," he assured her, and kissed her again to prove it.

From some distance away the faint sound of a car could be heard approaching in the night silence. Robbie MacLeod bringing the McEwans back! A tiny shadow crossed Nerissa's happiness.

"Duncan, about Fiona . . ."

"What about Fiona, darling?"

She felt suddenly nervous, shy, but it had to be said. "Didn't you have some sort of understanding with her father, in connection with his loan to you?"

"Nothing that concerned Fiona," he told her, a little frown riding his brow. "This visit of the McEwans is to mark the end of my financial arrangement with Sir Douglas. I made the last repayment just last week."

Her heart lightened. "Was that why you went over to see him?"

"It was. I felt that the final settlement after such a harmonious contract called for a personal visit. I've grown to like and admire Sir Douglas and his wife very much. They're both so kind-hearted and generous, so sincere. It's a pity that the same can't be said of their daughter. But they're overindulgent parents, and Fiona takes advantage of it."

"Yet you and she . . ." Nerissa began in protest.

Duncan shook his head at her reprovingly. "I won't try to pretend that I've led a celibate life, darling, but I swear this to you: I've never made any promises to Fiona—or any other woman—that I didn't intend to keep. Nor have I ever taken from a woman what wasn't freely offered." The sound of the car, though still a little way off, was growing louder. "We must tell them that we're going to be married," he said. "When shall it be, my love? I'm afraid it's quite pointless expecting me to wait long. If I could perform the ceremony myself we'd be married this very evening, so that I could carry off my bride and have my way with her."

In the flickering firelight she looked at him tenderly. "You need not wait, Duncan, you know that."

He laughed fondly. "Temptress! But I will not be lured—cost me what it may!"

Nerissa lowered her eyes. "Do you imagine it will cost *me* nothing?"

He laughed again, this time in triumph. "You are a shameless hussy! Oh, what a wonderful life we shall have together."

They kissed again, their bodies quickening with a flame of desire that threatened to consume them. Then as they heard the car draw up outside, they broke apart and stood up. Hand in hand, they waited to face the returning guests.

THE NEW NAME IN LOVE STORIES

Six new titles every month bring you the best in romance. Set all over the world, exciting and brand new stories about people falling in love:

THE NEW NAME IN LOVE STORIES

Silhouette Romance

THE NEW NAME IN LOVE STORIES

Silhouette *Romance*

EXCITING MEN,
EXCITING PLACES, HAPPY ENDINGS...

Contemporary romances for today's women

If there's room in your life for a little more romance,
SILHOUETTE ROMANCES are for you.

And you won't want to miss a single one so start
your collection now.

Each month, six very special love stories will be yours
from SILHOUETTE.

27938 9	WHISPER WIND Sondra Stanford No.112	75p
27939 7	WINTER BLOSSOM Dixie Browning No.113	75p
27940 0	PAINT ME RAINBOWS Fern Michaels No.114	75p
27942 7	AGAINST THE WIND Meredith Lindley No.116	75p
27943 5	MANHATTAN MASQUERADE Joanna Scott No.117	75p

All these books are available at your local bookshop or newsagent, or can be ordered direct from the publisher. Just tick the titles you want and fill in the form below.
Prices and availability subject to change without notice.

SILHOUETTE BOOKS, P.O. Box 11, Falmouth, Cornwall.

Please send cheque or postal order, and allow the following for postage and packing:

U.K. – 40p for one book, plus 18p for the second book, and 13p for each additional book ordered up to a £1.49 maximum.

B.F.P.O. and EIRE – 40p for the first book, plus 18p for the second book, and 13p per copy for the next 7 books, 7p per book thereafter.

OTHER OVERSEAS CUSTOMERS – 60p for the first book, plus 18p per copy for each additional book.

Name ....

Address ....

....